SMALL KINGDOMS
& OTHER STORIES

BOOKS BY CHARLAINE HARRIS

SMALL KINGDOMS
& OTHER STORIES

CHARLAINE HARRIS

Published by JABberwocky Literary Agency, Inc.

SMALL KINGDOMS AND OTHER STORIES

This paperback edition published in 2019 by
JABberwocky Literary Agency, Inc.

The stories included in this collection were originally published in the
following issues of *Ellery Queen Mystery Magazine*: "Small Kingdoms" in
November 2013, "Sarah Smiles" in September/October 2014, "Small Chances" in
September/October 2016, and "Small Signs" in November/December 2017.

Cover design by Tiger Bright Studios

Paperback ISBN 978-1-625673-78-7
Ebook ISBN 978-1-625673-77-0

http://www.awfulagent.com/ebooks

Contents

SMALL KINGDOMS

THE ORIGIN OF ANNE DEWITT was as random as most ideas are. I noticed one day that I washed myself in the same order every day. Face, then arms, etc. I wondered how many little routines we employ daily without being aware of them. Since I'm a writer, I then wondered what would happen if those routines were violently interrupted. Most of us wouldn't be able to cope with the shock.

But what if we were?

What if one woman was more than capable of defending herself with vigor?

It would have to be a woman with a blameless job and reputation—an orderly and disciplined woman. Hmmm. How had she acquired that discipline, that physical and mental toughness?

Gradually the world of "Small Kingdoms" began to take shape. I decided Anne needed a partner, and Holt Halsey was born.

I've now written several short stories about Anne DeWitt (initially known as Twyla Burnside) in the past few years, and I've thoroughly enjoyed writing every one. With each new story, I've tried to show a different side of Anne. I hope you enjoy her adventures. And I hope she's not the principal of your child's school.

On this particular spring Tuesday, Anne DeWitt was thrown off her regular schedule. Between brushing her teeth and putting on her foundation, she had to kill a man.

Most mornings, Anne was as accurate as a precision watch. Between the moment she rolled out of bed and the moment she got into her car, attractively groomed and dressed, Anne used a total of forty-five minutes. Following a fifteen-minute drive, during which she reviewed the day to come, Anne walked in the front doors of Travis High School at ten minutes before eight o'clock. Her secretary had better, by God, be sitting behind her own desk when Anne's heels clicked on the office floor.

But this Tuesday morning was not like most mornings, due to the short struggle and the longer effort of body disposal.

On the drive to work, she figured he'd scaled the roof while she was asleep, broken in a dormer window in the attic, and let down the attic steps while she was in the shower. (She'd noticed some specks on the carpet under the attic opening. Insulation?) Anne wasn't pleased that she hadn't foreseen this possibility, but she tried not to be too hard on herself either. A woman had to sleep. A shower made noise.

It was her fault, however, that she hadn't included the attic windows in her security system. She'd rectify that immediately.

It was Anne's good luck that she was looking in the mirror. If she hadn't been, she might have missed the flicker of movement as he came through the bathroom door, might not have realized the man was there until the wire cinched around her neck.

It was the would-be killer's bad luck that Anne was standing before the mirror naked, trimming a few errant hairs in her bangs, scissors in her hands. She pivoted instantly, her knees bent, and drove the sharp points upward into his throat, the two blades sinking in with a minimum of effort. Anne never bought inferior steel. Anne's hand came away, leaving the scissor blades in the double wound to minimize the inevitable leakage.

As a bonus, the dying man landed on the cotton bathmat with its no-slip rubber backing, which soaked up the trickles of blood.

Anne squatted by the body as the man died and looked at him intently. She was mildly surprised to discover she knew him: Bert Sawyer, her neighbor of two months, who'd moved in two doors west. He'd come over to borrow her jumper cables a week before. Anne spared a moment to think about that as she got the extra shower curtain liner, still in its packaging, from the bathroom linen closet.

She assumed "Bert" had had backers. They'd taken time to set this up, time and money. If Bert had been acting on his own, his preparation was even more impressive. This had been a carefully thought-out plan. None of the kids at Travis High School would have recognized their principal as she smiled at the failure of this plan, at her victory.

But it had been a victory by too narrow a margin. Anne's smile faded as she called herself to task. She was alive only because Bert had made stupid choices.

Why hadn't he attacked while she was asleep? Why had he waited until daylight, until she was clearly up and about? She stared down at the body, tempted to give it a kick. She was pretty damn irritated about losing the scissors.

A glance at her wall clock told her she was already running five minutes late, and there was a small spot of blood on her left shoulder. Dammit! She stepped back in the shower and washed herself off in case there were specks she hadn't noticed, careful not to get her hair wet since she'd already styled it for the day. She didn't want to spend the extra time to repeat the process.

As the water beat down, she thought hard about her next step. She was tempted to leave the body where it was until she came home from work, but there was always the chance that they (if there was a "they") would call the police, concoct some story that might compel the police to check out the inside of her house. *Heard screams...saw smoke...think someone's broken in...*any of those might make a conscientious cop insist on checking out the interior.

Anne puffed out her cheeks in exasperation as she completed her makeup. No, she had to do a certain amount of cleanup. Now she would be late, no doubt about it, and her record at this job had been as perfect as her record at her previous employment. Son of a bitch.

Her jaw set in a grim line, Anne pulled on rubber gloves and removed the plastic liner from its packaging. Anyone might use rubber gloves to clean, just as anyone might keep an extra shower curtain liner. Right? Hindered by the small floor space, Anne (who was very lean and athletic) managed to roll the body and the bathmat onto the clear plastic sheet and began securing it from the feet up, using duct tape from a fresh roll.

She left the scissors in the man's throat with a pang of true regret. She'd looked at many pairs of scissors before she'd selected those, and she'd used them exclusively to trim hair. That was why they'd maintained their great edge.

Well, she thought, *it was worth it.* She'd wiped off the handles, of course. She was sure any tiny snips of her hair that might have adhered to the blades would be too degraded by the time the body was found to be of any use to criminalists. In time, she'd acquire some more scissors for the rare self-trim job. Before she covered the dead man's face, she took another look.

Like Anne's, Bert Sawyer's hair was thick, though his was sable brown, several shades darker than hers. She wondered if Bert's hair was dyed, like hers; probably. She had another sudden thought, and pushed aside the would-be killer's hair in a couple of spots close to his ears. Huh. He'd had plastic surgery. She turned his face to the overhead light again, really concentrating on its contours, but there'd been so many faces in those ten years she'd run the school at her previous job.

And that had to be why he'd come here.

Anne deployed the duct tape until Bert Sawyer was encased and leak-proof. She cast a critical eye around the bathroom. There was no blood visible to the naked eye on the vanity or the mirror, but she ran a washrag over them nonetheless. All the while, she puzzled over

Bert Sawyer's true identity. But she dismissed her concerns after a glance at her watch; twenty minutes late, and the body to dispose of!

She called her secretary. "Christy, I'm running late today," she said. Anne's policy was never to apologize for things she couldn't have prevented.

"You are?" Christy, the doughy, fiftyish school secretary, couldn't hide her astonishment. "You're sick? Oh, I hope you haven't had an accident?"

Anne said, "My car wouldn't start. It's running now, but I'm behind."

"No problem," said Christy reassuringly.

Anne tried not to snarl at the phone. Of *course* the disruption of her routine was no problem for Christy; but it certainly was to Anne. "I'll be in as soon as I can. The Meachams aren't due for another forty-five minutes."

"Right," Christy said. "Oh, and Coach Halsey is in here. I'll tell him to come back."

The baseball coach had never come to her office for a one-on-one before. Anne almost asked what Holt Halsey wanted, but it was hardly Christy's job to find out, if the information hadn't been volunteered. "Do that," Anne said pleasantly and evenly.

She went into the bedroom to put on her underwear and went back to the bathroom to check her shoulder-length hair, stepping over the corpse on her way. Then

Anne put on the outfit she'd laid out the night before: gray trouser suit, well-cut, with a darker gray silk blouse. Garnet earrings and a necklace with a garnet pendant, small and tasteful. But then she put on sneakers, grabbing the black pumps she'd selected to go with the outfit.

Anne bounded down the stairs, passed through the gleaming kitchen with its block of sharp knives, and opened the door to the garage. After placing her high heels on the floorboard of the passenger-side front, Anne opened her trunk, spreading out another plastic sheet (just in case). There was a cheap yellow rain slicker, the kind you could buy in a hanging pouch from the rack of any dollar store, hanging on a hook by the back door. Anne pulled it on, carefully drawing the hood over her chestnut hair. She went back up the stairs to her bathroom to grab the ankles of the plastic-shrouded corpse. Tugging carefully, steadily, digging in her feet, Anne dragged the body down the stairs.

Bert Sawyer's head bumped against each wooden step. Anne, who'd heard much worse noises, ignored the sound.

Getting Bert into the trunk was tricky, but nothing Anne hadn't done before. When the body was completely inside, she pulled off the cheap slicker and stuffed it in with the body. She went into the house one final time to grab her purse and give her hair a once-over look in the mirror. Finally—finally!—she was on her way to work. She'd been thinking while she stuffed Bert in the trunk, and she'd thought of a good spot to dispose of him.

The winding roads and pleasantly rolling hills relaxed Anne, as always. The four-lane was moderately busy, but due to Anne's unwilling delay, there were fewer cars than usual. When she got close to the spot she'd chosen, she drove in the slow lane until the road was clear. Then she whipped right and went down a gravel road just wide enough for her car. Luckily, it hadn't rained recently, or she would have had to make a different choice. But Bert would molder nicely out here. It would only get warmer and damper every week now that spring had arrived in North Carolina.

At the end of this service road was some sort of electrical relay tower, surrounded by a high gated fence liberally posted with warnings. The gate was heavily padlocked, which was fine with Anne, since she had no interest in gaining entrance. Her car was far enough into the woods to be invisible from the four-lane, and she maneuvered Bert's body out of the trunk with the facility of experience. As a bonus, the gravel road was slightly raised for drainage, so she was able to roll the plastic bundle into the forest and then drag it through the pines until it could not be seen from the gravel track. After leaving the body behind a copse, Anne grabbed a fallen branch. On her way back to the car, she swept away the swath the passage of the corpse had cut through the winter leaves and pine needles. She was glad the temperature this morning was in the high fifties; she didn't want to work up a sweat.

Good enough, Anne thought, as she stood by her car brushing her jacket and her pants. She swung the car around on the apron before the fence, and when she returned to the four-lane she stayed back in the tree line until the road was clear.

It was less than two miles to Travis High School, where Anne had worked for four years; two as assistant principal, two as principal. After she'd parked in her designated parking space, she exchanged her sneakers for the high heels.

She looked up at the big wall clock as she entered the school lobby. She was now fifty minutes late. *Damn* Bert Sawyer, and whoever had recruited him. Anne shoved the anger aside. She would have to think seriously about Bert and his garrote later. No one had tried to kill her for three years.

For now, her head should be in its proper place. This school was her kingdom; she was its ultimate ruler. She relaxed because she was within the walls of her domain.

She got her second surprise for the day when she opened the door to the outer office, Christy Strunk's domain. Coach Holt Halsey was still waiting for her. This surprise wasn't exactly either good or bad; but it was unprecedented. Her respect for the baseball coach, who'd come on board two years ago, was not only based on Halsey's winning record, but also on the fact that Halsey seemed to solve his own problems in a rational way.

Christy looked at her with some apology, and Anne understood that she'd tried to get the coach to return later, with no success. Anne said, "Good morning, Christy."

A few brisk steps took her abreast of Halsey, who'd risen from his chair. It didn't bother Anne at all to look up at him. She was not intimidated by large men. But she hesitated before using his first name, since she'd never done so. "Holt, how long do you need? I have less than ten minutes, if that'll do the job."

The coach nodded. "I only need a few minutes," he said. She walked over to the inner door, the door to her office, with her name on it. She loved the sight of it, no matter how many times she passed it. That she'd been born neither "Anne" nor "DeWitt" made no difference to her pleasure.

"I'll hold your calls, Ms. DeWitt," Christy said unnecessarily. That was SOP in this office.

"Come in," Anne said. Christy had been in to turn on the light and deposit her messages, but everything was as Anne had left it the evening before. She checked automatically as she moved behind the desk to put her purse in its drawer. She'd carefully arranged the office to make it seem as though she'd led a complete life. There were two pictures of her parents, one of her sister, and one of her deceased husband.

None of these people existed. Of course, she had had parents, but she'd never met them. She'd never been married. To the best of her knowledge, she didn't have a sister. "Have a seat, Holt," Anne said, pulling out her own chair and sitting. There was a handful of call slips lined up beside her mouse pad. It had taken her two weeks to break Christy of the habit of telling her about each call as she entered the office. She allowed the fearful idea that she might have to leave, that there might be another attempt—who had the would-be assassin alerted when he'd tracked her down? With grim determination, she shoved this conjecture back to the corner of her mind.

Coach Halsey was sitting, elbows on knees, in one of the lightly padded chairs positioned in front of Anne's neat desk. Holt Halsey was a broad-shouldered man, a couple of inches over six feet, and he had a face that might have been chiseled out of granite. He wasn't unattractive in a rough-hewn way, but he didn't work that attraction, and he didn't show a lot of emotion. Anne liked both qualities.

"Clay Meacham is a problem," Holt Halsey said, without further ado.

"Odd you should bring him up. His parents are coming in right after I finish talking to you."

The coach's flinty face managed to convey his opinion of the Meachams in a precise, economical tightening of the lips.

Brandon and Elaine Meacham, the parents of Travis High's star pitcher, were active in the Baseball Boosters Club, and they spent a lot of time volunteering at other school activities. Clay was their only child. They didn't miss a single opportunity to support and promote the handsome junior.

If Clay had been as good a young man as he was talented, Anne would have thoroughly approved. Clay's academic and athletic glory was the school's (and therefore her) glory. But Clay was not a good young man, and his judgment was deeply flawed.

"What's he done?" she asked.

"He was messing with Hazel Reid."

Their eyes met while Anne absorbed the implications. She considered wasting time with things a normal woman would have said, like, "How is she?" or "Should we call the police?" None of that was on the table: if it had been, Holt would have led with the worst news. Hazel Reid was mentally and emotionally handicapped. But she was also a physically mature sixteen. Anne said, "How far did it go?"

"He'd taken her shirt off," the coach said.

"Where?"

"In the woods in back of the school. If she hadn't been wearing bright pink, I wouldn't have spotted them."

"So, after school. But on school property."

"Yeah."

"Why wasn't she on her bus?" Hazel was supposed to catch the vehicle derisively called "the short bus" to her home.

"Her mom was here for teacher conferences. She'd parked Hazel on the bench outside to wait. Clay saw her when he was walking to his car after practice. I guess he was in a bad mood. Or maybe a good one."

"Does he know you know?" she asked.

"Not for sure. I called him on his cell phone, asked him if he'd seen Hazel in the parking lot, her mom was looking for her."

Anne checked the list of phone calls she'd gotten that morning, and Mrs. Reid wasn't on it. "Hazel didn't tell," Anne said.

"I don't think she minded," the coach said. "But she's not mentally capable to consent or refuse."

"Noted," Anne said. She thought for a moment, and Coach Halsey let her.

Her previous job had been far tougher than this one, and when she'd left it so abruptly, she'd sworn to herself she wouldn't ever get so invested again. But here she was, thinking of Travis High and its reputation.

Did Anne care about each individual student? No. But this was her turf, and she would protect it. She would make it as perfect as she could. When she looked up at the rugged, impenetrable face of her baseball coach, she surprised a look almost of . . . sympathy. And for a second . . .

"Do I know you?" she asked, with no premeditation.

He smiled. It was like watching rock move. "It's time for the Meachams to get here. I'll hear from you later." It wasn't quite a question.

"You will," she said, and stood up. They eyed each other for a moment. It was as though Holt Halsey was willing her to realize something. But then he turned to go, and she had to change gears to deal with Clay's parents.

The Meachams weren't anything special, in Anne's expert estimation. Brandon, handsome like his son but not as mean, might look at other women but he never touched. His wife, Elaine, a former pageant queen, made a creditable effort to conceal the fact that she didn't give a shit about anyone else's child but her own. She would clap for another child's achievement, she would tell the other moms how much she admired their progeny, but in truth she believed the sun shone out of Clay's ass.

All in all, Anne couldn't feel surprised that Clay had no sense of guilt in taking advantage of a handicapped girl. He was sure that everything he did was fine, simply because he, Clay, wanted to do it.

"Ms. DeWitt," Elaine Meacham said, flashing her broad white smile. "Thanks for making the time to see us today."

"Of course. What do we need to talk about this morning?" Anne asked, trying to cut through the pleasantries. She gestured them to the chairs in front of her desk, took her own seat again.

"I saw you at the last game," Brandon said, to make sure she knew he appreciated her. "I know the kids think it's really cool that you go to all the sporting events."

"Of course I do," Anne said. *This is my school,* she thought. *I'm going to go to everything I physically can.* She adopted her fallback face: pleasant, but not encouraging. Not only did she have to think about Coach Halsey's tale, the pile of paperwork in the in-basket wasn't going to take care of itself. She had two other meetings scheduled during the day too, one with a prospective temporary replacement for the enormously pregnant Spanish teacher, and one with a vendor who wanted the school to switch to his software system in the chemistry lab. The vendor would ask her out for a drink after work: she would refuse him. She was going to have to be more forceful in her refusal this time.

Barely able to restrain some manifestation of her boredom and her itching desire to get to the work on her desk, Anne had to sit through a few more platitudes before Brandon got down to brass tacks.

"Principal DeWitt—Anne—we hope the school will help Clay achieve his goal," Brandon said very seriously.

"Which goal is that?" Anne worked to keep her voice neutral. She was thinking of how much she'd like to kick Clay Meacham's ass. The enormity of the boy's offense was sinking into her psyche. She didn't even want to imagine the headlines, the disgrace of the school, the navel-gazing that would inevitably follow the exposure of Clay's little after-hours adventure with the hapless Hazel Reid. Anne found herself thinking wistfully of some of the more inventive punishments she'd employed at her previous job.

Instead of getting to the point, the Meachams began the litany of what Clay had meant to the school: class president, star athlete, honor roll, captain of the debate team. "And what goal would that be?" Anne prompted again, when she felt her impatience building to a dangerous level.

Cut off in mid-flow, Elaine looked comically surprised. "I'm sorry?" she said.

"I'm very well aware of Clay's position at Travis," Anne said evenly. "Can you tell me what you think Clay needs from this school?"

"Sure," Brandon said. "Sure. I'm sorry, we got kind of carried away, like parents tend to do." He smiled at Anne in what he surely felt was an ingratiating manner, though he couldn't suppress the snap of irritation in his voice.

She tried not to let her shoulders heave in a sigh of exasperation, but maybe the lines of her face conveyed her strong desire to extract some specifics.

"It's his senior film." Elaine again bathed Anne in the radiance of her brilliant smile.

"Clay isn't in the drama department's film class," Anne said. "I'm afraid I don't follow you."

"He needs a film to send to recruiters. Clay's such an outstanding pitcher, we want to be sure he's placed at the right college, with a good scholarship. So he needs a film to send out to athletic departments early next school year. We've got some examples." Elaine extracted some DVD cases from her purse and set them on the edge of Anne's desk.

"So you'll hire someone to film Clay's games?" Anne said, not reaching for the DVD cases.

"We were kind of hoping that we could use clips from the school's game films," Elaine explained. She kept the smile in place. "It seems like a shame to duplicate effort."

She meant it was a shame for the Meachams to spend their own money. Anne had wondered how Meacham Motors was doing in this recession. She thought she'd just learned the answer.

It was true that the school lined up an employee or some astute volunteer parent to film every baseball game—and all the other sports events too, of course. This was invaluable as a teaching tool, the coaches assured her.

The politically correct response would be that of course Clay's recruiting film could be composed of clips from the game recordings, and Coach Halsey would be happy to help with such an effort. But what if Clay's recent misdeed came to light? Wouldn't the school suffer, especially if it had offered this extra support to an athlete who'd proved to be a rotten, degraded, egg? While Anne allowed herself a lot of moral leeway—she had no problem killing people who attacked her—she did deplore Clay's self-indulgence and poor judgment in attempting to seduce a girl who would never be an adult mentally or emotionally.

"I'll discuss it with Coach Halsey," Anne said briskly. "Who would you expect to do the work involved in editing the film, excerpting Clay's pitches? I'm assuming you'd also want the times he comes up to bat included in the recruiting film. I don't know what would be involved, but I'm assuming you two do?"

"Well," Brandon said, doing his best to look as if he weren't being pushy, "I think we were hoping that since Clay is the best pitcher Travis High's ever had, and him going to a good school to pitch would be a great feather for Coach Halsey's cap . . ."

"So you think Coach Halsey should do this work."

Elaine spread her hands. "Well, we were just hoping! Since he's fairly new here, still making his name . . ."

Anne knew how many hours Halsey put in on his job, for slim money. "It's baseball season now," she said, as if they needed to be reminded. "I don't know how much time the coach could devote to doing this for one player, no matter how gifted. Of course we all want to see Clay succeed, and we want him to play for the college of his choice. Has he told you where he'd like to go?" She put on a somewhat brighter smile and got up, signaling the end of the interview.

Somewhat bewildered, the Meachams rose too. "He was thinking of the University of Arkansas—they're in the top five. Or Louisiana. Maybe UCLA, though we don't want him that far from home."

Three top baseball programs. The Meachams were aiming very high. Was Clay really that good? She would ask Coach Halsey.

Anne finally got the Meachams out of the office with promises to "get back with them" after talking to Coach Halsey. Then she returned the calls on Christy's list. Then she dove into the paperwork. Before she knew it, the bell rang for first lunch, the sophomore seating.

Normally, Anne would have brought a salad to eat at her desk, or even shared the students' meal choices in the cafeteria, though that was strictly an exercise in morale boosting. But today, she went home for lunch, as she was careful to do at least once a week, though never on the same day. Her house, tidy and spruce with its fresh paint and neat yard, had an interior air of slight dishevelment, like a bed made crookedly. Her breakfast cereal bowl still sat by the sink, unrinsed. Upstairs, the bathroom looked curiously incomplete since the bathmat was missing. Her makeup was not aligned on its tray. Her pajamas were still lying across the bench at the foot of her bed. But Anne left these little signals of disruption. She'd take care of them after more pressing matters.

She took her gun with her when she let down the attic stairs and ascended them.

She didn't seriously believe there was another assailant in her attic. But then, she hadn't expected the first one either. That failure was bitter to Anne, whose job in the past had been to teach others to be masters of close fighting. Quicker, smarter, faster, tougher, able to take more stress and dodge more punishment than other human beings. And many people who'd passed through Anne's hands had become wonderful killers.

Standing in her own attic, seeing the evidence of last night's intrusion, Anne was bitterly aware she had failed. She'd been lulled by her artificial life into an equally artificial sense of security. In her own home, her lack of readiness had come very close to getting her killed.

There were three dormer windows in the attic, which was painted and floored. Its walls were lined with everything that belonged in a storage space. There was a modest box of Christmas decorations underneath a wreath hung on a wall hook. There was a box of old pictures in aged frames, which any casual visitor would assume were ancestors of Anne's.

Well, the long-dead faces belonged to someone's ancestors, but not hers, as far as she knew. She was proud of a trunk of fake memorabilia that had belonged to her fake dead husband. There was an antique quilt inside, among the report cards and trophies, a quilt that must have been stitched by someone's grandmother; it might as well have been "Brad's." There was an old rickety rocking chair by the trunk, just the kind of chair such a grandmother might have rocked in as she quilted. There was a crate packed with a very old set of china, and one full of the sort of scholarly books Anne DeWitt might have collected over the course of her academic progress: Jacobean poets, theories of education, the psychology of leadership. The attic was as carefully staged as the rest of the house.

Bert Sawyer had come in through the west dormer. The dormers faced the road, but in the wee hours of the morning there was not likely to be anyone up or about on this quiet residential cul-de-sac, one carved out of the woods. The house between Anne's and Sawyer's belonged to the Westhovens, and they had left for Florida the previous week. Maybe that was why Sawyer had chosen the previous night for his move on Anne.

The pane on the window had been cut out and removed, and cool spring air flooded the attic, carrying the pleasant scent of budding plants.

Obviously, Bert had ascertained that the dormers weren't hooked up to the alarm system. He must have made a preliminary trip to her roof on some previous night. She'd have to figure out how he'd scaled it, because she didn't see a rope and there was no ladder leaning against the eaves, for godsake. She thought about all these things as she noted the tiny signs of his presence in her attic; the dust on the trunk had been smudged, probably by his butt as he sat on it to wait for the sound of her shower running. There was a small ring in the dust too. Anne decided he'd had a tiny flashlight, and he'd used it to check out the story her attic was supposed to tell. It must have been in his pocket when she dumped him.

The woman she'd formerly been would have learned how to replace her own glass, but Anne DeWitt would not do such a thing. She decided to tell the repairman that a bird must have flown into the window, and she'd found it broken. Of course, Anne DeWitt would have cleaned the mess up immediately. Anne found the pane of glass, leaning carefully against a wall. She put it on the floor and stomped on it. Then she fetched a broom and dustpan from the kitchen and swept up the fragments. She called the handyman that helped her out with things Anne DeWitt couldn't do. He agreed to come the next afternoon at five.

Anne would wait a couple of days to call the alarm system people.

After another, more thorough, cleaning of the bathroom, Anne had only time to grab a granola bar to eat on the way back to school. Her stomach growled in protest, and she promised herself she'd have a good dinner.

On her way back to Travis High, she saw a pickup truck emerging from the gravel road to the electric tower, the spot where she'd dumped Bert Sawyer's body. Every nerve in her body went on the alert as she passed the road, and the truck pulled out behind her.

She recognized it. It was Holt Halsey's.

He drove behind her all the way back to the school. She went to the administrative parking lot, and he went left to park by the gym complex.

There was nothing Anne could do about the coach that afternoon. He was a riddle, for sure, and one she'd better solve sooner rather than later. It was no coincidence that he'd gone down that obscure track; and she didn't believe it was a coincidence that he'd emerged from it just when she was approaching.

He'd found the body.

He hadn't told anyone.

After an hour had passed, she knew he wasn't going to.

The meeting with the salesman, her last of the day, was over by five o'clock. Christy was itching to leave, opening and closing drawers on her desk with annoying frequency, as Anne could see (and hear) through her open office door. When this salesman (she mentally called him The Jerk) visited, she always left her door open. She didn't want to have to break his arm, which she had been sorely tempted to do more than once.

The second she stood up to conduct The Jerk out, Christy was out of the door like a shot. The Jerk took the opportunity to put his hand on her arm. "Please reconsider. I'd love to take you to dinner at the lake," he said, smiling his most sincere smile.

Anne looked at him, thinking about pulling out his teeth one by one.

"Sorry," said Holt's deep voice from the doorway. "The principal and I have things to discuss this evening."

The Jerk covered his chagrin well—after all, he was a salesman—and Holt and Anne regarded each other. There was so much texture and complexity to that look she could have worn it like a sweater. When The Jerk was gone, and the school was quiet and empty around them, Holt said, "Well, you had a busy morning. No wonder you were late."

And Anne heard herself saying, "Who *are* you?"

This was a talk that had to be private, but Anne was not about to go to Holt's house, and she didn't want him in hers, not yet. They drove separately to a restaurant that was nearly empty at this time of day. They asked to be seated on the patio, which had just opened for the season. It was almost too cool to sit in the open air in the late afternoon, but Anne was willing to be a little chilly if it meant no one would be close to them.

After they'd ordered drinks and plate of nachos, he said, "Holt isn't the name I was born with, but I expect to use it for some time. I know you're Twyla Burnside. My little brother was in your tenth class."

Anne considered all this while their drinks came. "So you know all about the event."

"The one that got you fired? Yes."

"Why are you here, at Travis?"

"I did the same training, but in a different location," he said. "The guy in charge was as tough as you can imagine. He was coming up a couple of years before you got your job. David Angola."

She nodded. David Angola had saved her ass at the secret hearing. "I lost one person in almost every class," she said. "Until the tenth class, they always considered it the price of doing business. It was my job to make sure the grads were the best my school could produce. They had to pass the tests I set. Of course, the tests were rigorous. I would fail in my mandate if they weren't as challenging as I could possibly devise... to ensure the grads were completely prepared for extreme duress and with extraordinary survival skills. Until my tenth year as an instructor, one loss a year was acceptable." She shook her head. "And that year, the lost student was the one with connections."

Holt smiled, very slightly. "You have a huge reputation, even now. David himself said he was a pussy, compared to you."

She smiled, a wry twist of the lips. "That's a huge compliment, coming from David. That woman's brain aneurysm could have gone at any time. You can't tell me it gave because of 'undue rigor' or 'borderline cruelty.' Her bad luck, and mine. Her mom had a lot of pull."

Holt's face held no judgment. "They give you the new identity when they fired you?"

"Complete with references."

"Me too."

She raised an interrogative eyebrow.

"Shot the wrong person," he said. "But it was a righteous mistake."

She absorbed that. "Okay," she said. "And you're here because?"

"David heard some people were coming after you. You got some enemies."

"No one's tried for three years."

"Right before I got to Travis, huh?"

"Yeah. This guy was waiting in my car after I chaperoned the senior prom."

"Garrote?"

"No, knife. The man this morning, he had a garrote."

Their nachos came then, and they ate with some appetite.

"David actually sent you here?" she asked, when she'd eaten all she could.

"When they cut me loose with a coach persona, David gave me a call. He thought this might be a good place for me to land."

"I've never felt like you were watching me. Are you that good?"

"I didn't need to watch you too closely. You're great with your cover. This morning, when you came in I could tell you'd broken your routine because something had happened, and I got a little whiff of blood from your hair."

Anne was intensely angry at herself. She should have taken fifteen more minutes to re-wash and re-style her hair.

"So you figured out..."

"If I assumed someone had gone for you, I knew where I would have dumped him. I figured I might as well check."

"You're cool with this."

"Sure," he said, surprised. "I had a look at him. Chuck Wallis. He was the brother of . . ."

The name triggered a switch. "Jeremy Wallis. He died in the fifth class. So. Now what?"

"Now we figure out what to do about that little shit Clay."

She smiled. It was not a pleasant smile. It was Twyla Burnside's smile, not Anne DeWitt's. She would have to rebury herself in her new character all over again, but it felt so good to let Twyla out. "I think we need to put the fear into him."

"The fear of God?"

"The fear of us. Oh, by the way, let me tell you why the Meachams came to my office this morning. It'll get you in the mood."

The next afternoon Coach Halsey kept Clay after practice. The kid was tired, because the practice had been extra tough, but he didn't complain. Clay knew that Coach Halsey hated whiners. After he finished the extra exercises the coach had outlined for him, he trudged out to his car. It was dark by now, and he called his mom to let her know he'd be late. He was thoughtful like that, no matter what people said.

At first, Clay didn't know what was suddenly poking him in his head. Something hard and small. He felt the presence of someone behind him. "Hey, jerk," he said angrily, beginning to turn. "What the hell?"

"What the hell indeed," said a strange voice, a voice as metallic as the gun that tapped his cheek. "Keep a polite tongue in your mouth. If you want to keep your tongue."

Since nothing awful had ever happened to Clay Meacham, he didn't realize the genuine seriousness of this moment. "Listen, asshole, you don't know who you're messing with," he growled.

He was instantly slapped by something that felt soft but weighty. It stung. He staggered. "You're asking for it!" he yelled.

And then he couldn't yell anymore, because he was seized by two strong arms and gagged and blindfolded by two deft hands. As Clay's fear began to swell and explode in his brain, he was bundled into his own car, his keys were extracted from his pocket, and the two hooded figures drove him down county roads and dirt tracks, deep into the woods.

Once he was on his knees, the metallic voice said, "Clay. We need you to be the best you can be. If you're going to represent all of us when you're in college, you need to be bulletproof. If you're going to be bulletproof,

31

you have to stop molesting women who aren't able to say yes or no. You have to stop being a taker. Because someday, someone will call you on it. And then you'll let us down. I can't tell you how much we don't want that to happen. So, Clay, you need to tell us now, about what you've done before, things you're not going to do in the future." Though his first confession had to be coaxed out of him, Clay found himself telling the two invisible presences everything. Everything he'd ever done to people, people smaller and weaker and less handsome than himself. And he'd done a lot.

After an hour, he was sorry for it all.

By the time Clay got home that night, he flinched whenever his parents asked him a question. He told them repeatedly he'd had a bad day, and he only wanted to go to bed. When they demanded to know why his face was so reddened, he said a ball had hit him at practice. He went to his bedroom as though he was dragging a chain behind him, and Elaine and Brandon were too worried to remember to ask Clay if the coach had mentioned working on the recruiting film for him.

Clay only went to school because he was scared to be at home by himself after his parents had left for their jobs. At school, he jumped when his friends slung their arms around him, punched him in the shoulder, and in general acted like kids on the cusp of becoming men. For the first time in his life, Clay knew what it was like to be weak. To be lesser.

When his best buddy strolled past Hazel Reid's table in the lunchroom, his fist raised to pound on the table to make Hazel jump (a trick that never grew old with Clay's friends), Clay caught that fist and said, simply, "No. Not any more."

"Awww, man," the friend said, but he'd heard the pronouncement of the most popular boy in school. Not any more.

Clay turned to leave the lunchroom and saw Principal DeWitt standing, straight and lean as an arrow, about two yards away. He was seized by an almost uncontrollable impulse to rush to her and tell her what had happened to him. Everyone said DeWitt was a smart woman and a good principal. She would be able to figure out who'd kidnapped him.

Or maybe not. There were so many candidates.

There were a lot of sins Clay Meacham had never thought twice about committing, sins of which he was now painfully aware. His eyes had been opened last night, even though he'd been blindfolded.

Clay was only seventeen, and he wasn't clear on how he was supposed to attain perfection, but the guidelines he'd been given last night had been pretty clear.

He saw the principal again that day, when she came to watch the team practice. That wasn't an uncommon occurrence. While Clay was waiting to come up to bat, he saw Coach Halsey look at Ms. DeWitt. It made Clay shiver. Clay'd been scared he'd pitch poorly that day, but now that he knew there'd be a price to pay if he failed, his focus was amazing.

After practice, Principal DeWitt drifted over to talk to Coach Halsey. After a second, Coach beckoned Clay over. He trotted over to the two adults.

"I hear you need a recruitment film," Coach Halsey said.

"My parents say I need one to send out next year, yessir," Clay said.

"I'm willing to help you make it, but I won't do all the work," Coach said. "You'll have to put in some hours helping me do other things, so I'll have some free time."

The old Clay would have been sullen about giving up anything to get something that was his due. The new Clay said, "Yessir. Just say when." He turned and went into the locker room.

"I think he's been turned around," Anne said.

"At least for now." Coach Halsey looked down at her. "Want to get dinner Saturday night?"

"I think so," she said, after a pause. "There are a few things we might want to talk about."

"Oh?"

"Sarah Toth's dad is hitting her."

"Well," Holt said. "We can't have that. She won't get the high test scores if she's being beaten at home."

"If she scores two points higher the next time she takes the SAT, it'll be a state record."

He smiled. No one else would have enjoyed that smile but Anne. "Then we'd better get cracking."

They both laughed, just a little. "By the way," Holt said. "What happened to the principal before you? You became assistant here the year before she killed herself, right?"

Anne nodded, her expression faintly regretful. "Mrs. Snyder was having sex in her office with a married teacher, Ted Cole. Christy overheard a conversation between them and came to me with it."

"Then it would have been all over the school in short order." He smiled. "Good job. Proactive."

Anne smiled back before she glanced down at her watch. "I have to be at my house to let the handyman in," she murmured. But she lingered for a moment. "Snyder almost didn't hire me. She was not a fan, from the first interview until the last. But the school board liked me. And the minute I saw Travis High, I knew it was a place where I could make a difference. Now..." She looked up at him and away, almost shyly. "Now there's no limit."

"No limit," he agreed, and they stood silent in the lowering sun, their long shadows streaking across the practice field.

SARAH SMILES

I DIDN'T WANT TO FOLLOW the pattern of my first Anne DeWitt story, so I cast about for another way of showing Anne doing what she's best at.

I wondered what Anne's past had been. She had been a teenager once and what was she like? Even then, she must have been smart and ruthless. How had her foster parents fared with someone like Anne in their house? When did she begin to realize she could manipulate events to make things go the way she wanted them to go?

How far did she go?

So in "Sarah Smiles," I switched things up a bit so you could all think about that.

Sarah Toth parked her car in the Travis High parking lot just in time to hear the first bell ring. She and her brother James exchanged a long look as they unbuckled their seat belts. "Isn't there any other way?" he asked her.

As she shook her head, her glossy braid whipped back and forth on her back like an animal's tail. "We've talked about this," she said, her voice flat. "Come on, bubba. We'll be late." James, whose first class was in the south wing, took off in that direction without looking back. More slowly, Sarah went to the main entrance. It was the oldest part of the school, and there were stairs up to the huge front door. She went up them awkwardly, and as she made her way in she could tell that other kids noticed her limp. The door to the left led to the outer room of the principal's office, where Christy the secretary reigned. The principal herself, Anne DeWitt, had emerged from her inner sanctum to watch the students flow into the building, as she did from time to time. Ms. DeWitt's face was always calm, always composed, and Sarah found it impossible to tell what the principal was thinking while she scanned the incoming teenagers. When their eyes met, Sarah nodded, because she was a polite and politic girl. She wasn't surprised when Principal DeWitt nodded back. Everyone on the faculty knew who Sarah was, a source of some pride to the girl. But Principal DeWitt wasn't the adult she was looking for this morning.

There. Mr. Mathis, the assistant principal, was standing at the T junction of the main hall and the entrance area, his invariable post in the morning. Sarah could feel him watching her as she limped past. She was sure his eyes followed her as she turned left to go to her first period class. World History was taught by Coach Holt Halsey, who was a surprisingly good teacher for a coach. Everyone—everyone in Sarah's world, that is, the students of Travis High, Colleton County, North Carolina—thought of Halsey, boys' baseball coach, as a little forbidding. He wouldn't put up with foolishness, but he was approachable about serious stuff, and he had the reputation of knowing everything about any student who took part in a sport, both boys and girls.

Sarah was decidedly non-athletic. She was a short,

slightly plump, seventeen-year-old senior, with unfashionably waist-length dull brown hair and an unfashionably curvy figure. Sarah wore glasses, though behind them were large blue eyes. She proudly flew the flag for the nerd camp. Sarah was very aware she was possibly the smartest student—maybe the smartest person, teachers included—at Travis High. But that didn't mean she was happy.

Sarah's brain was not on Coach Halsey's mind as he noted the girl's slow progress to her desk. While he taught the mostly bored first-period students about the Reign of Terror, he was trying to recall how many times he'd seen Sarah with bruises. When the bell rang at the end of the period, he stopped her as she made her way to the door. "Sarah, hold up," he said, his voice neither quiet nor loud.

Sarah paused, her eyes cast down. "Yessir?"

"Your leg?" the coach asked. He was a man of few words.

Sarah shrugged, not meeting his eyes. "I fell on the stairs," she said.

In the ensuing silence, Sarah's shoulders stiffened. Finally, her gaze met Coach Halsey's. He saw that her eyes were filled with rage. He hadn't expected that. It interested him. He sat down so he wouldn't be looming over the girl. He thought it might put her at ease. Halsey was well aware he made some people nervous.

Mostly, he was fine with that.

"You're going to take the SAT again in three weeks?" Halsey asked, after a glance at the calendar.

"Yessir," she said. "At least, I . . . I plan on doing that."

He didn't ask what might stop her.

"Just two points away from a school record," the coach observed. "We're proud of you. The honor you're bringing the school."

She smiled quite genuinely. "That's really nice of you, Coach. Thanks. 'Scuse me, I'm late." And then she scuttled—well, limped as quickly as she could—to her next class. Halsey noticed that Brian Vaughan was waiting to walk with her. Brian was tall, gawky, and had hair like a bird's nest. He was a good kid. Brian ran track—not with distinction, but with reliability. Halsey, who was excellent at sizing people up, thought Brian would have a pleasant life unless something crazy happened to him. Halsey knew more than anyone at Travis High suspected (anyone except the principal, Anne DeWitt) about the terrible things that could happen to people. He'd had a previous career that would make parents blanch if they discovered it.

Though he didn't often spend time in the teachers' lounge, Halsey got a cup of coffee there at lunchtime. Sarah's limp was the main topic of discussion that day, though everyone was being carefully oblique. Coach Halsey didn't join in the talk, but he listened intently.

"James seems okay," said the older mathematics teacher, very cautiously. "Moody, sure, but healthy." Sarah's brother was younger than her by two years, but he was tall and strong and an athlete.

Reading between the lines, Halsey interpreted that to mean that James had no appearance of being abused. Though all the faculty members knew that an abusive parent sometimes picked one child to be the punching bag, James's well-being made it a bit more plausible that Sarah was genuinely accident-prone.

"James doesn't seem very happy," Coach Redding said. James played football for Redding.

"James is a teenager," the younger biology teacher said. He was the most cynical person on the faculty. "Teenagers are unhappy by definition."

"That's simply not true," the calculus teacher said, giving the biology teacher an unfriendly look. She rose to get some more coffee. "They're as happy as they're allowed to be."

"I asked Sarah about her home life," said the school nurse, and there was a silence in the lounge. "She came to me because her arm was hurting. She said she'd fallen. But there was a mark on her upper arm, looked a lot like a grip mark."

The faculty members present all stared at the nurse, a middle-aged woman with a sweet face and a practical air about her. "And she said?" asked the older math teacher.

"She said everything was fine at home," the nurse said, and shrugged. "She said that her father grabbed her to keep her from falling off the front porch. What are you gonna do?"

There was a moment of silence. If Sarah would not confide in someone as trusted as the nurse, she would not confide in anyone, was the unspoken consensus. And if her brother James wanted to report what was happening to his sister—if anything was—he'd had plenty of opportunity. It was not a clear-cut situation. The previous principal, the one before Anne DeWitt, had made an accusation of abuse that had proved to be false, and they were all gun-shy as a result.

After the last bell of the day, Coach Halsey went to the principal's office. He was glad to see that the secretary had already left, because he wanted to talk to Anne DeWitt without Christy's sharp ears listening. He knocked on the doorframe of the inner office. Anne looked up from the pile of paperwork on her desk.

"More to fill out?"

"The government," she said tersely. Anne was in her thirties, young for a high school principal. She was lean and muscular and quietly attractive. When she'd been hired as assistant to the previous principal, the school board had been impressed not only with her steady and serious demeanor, but her glowing recommendations. Also, they'd figured that her status as a childless widow meant she would be free to put in long hours. When Principal Delia Snyder had committed suicide (a shocking and tragic loss), Anne had been a shoo-in to fill the post. The school board had no idea what a total package they were getting. Under another name, Anne DeWitt had trained government operatives at a secret camp. She had trained them to survive in extreme conditions. Naturally, a few students had failed her class by dying; Anne had made a few enemies during her service. Her new name, background, and occupation were fabrications she would maintain the rest of her life—a kind of severance package.

Holt Halsey, who'd graduated from a similar class, waited quietly while Anne took care of a few more forms. When she looked up and stacked the papers neatly, signaling she was ready to talk, Holt said, "We have a problem."

"Penny Carson?"

"No . . . wait, the Spanish teacher? What's she up to?"

"I saw her coming out of a liquor store in Candle Springs. Why go to a liquor store in another town unless you're buying a lot more than you should be consuming?" They both understood that the issue was not Penny

Carson's morals. The issue was the potential scandal and bad publicity for Travis High School if a teacher was discovered to be an alcoholic.

"So you might have to have a talk with her."

"Not on the basis of one out-of-town trip to a liquor store," Anne said briskly. "But I'm going to keep an eye on her."

Halsey nodded, accepting Anne's judgment. She'd been trained to evaluate hazardous situations, and she was usually very accurate. "Sarah Toth was limping today," he said without preamble. "She's getting beaten at home, but she won't talk about it. This is not the first time she's come to school with perceptible physical issues. And the SATs are in three weeks. I've never met her parents. Have you?"

"JimBee and Lizzy." Anne leaned back in her office chair. "Yes, I've had the pleasure." She crossed her legs, and Holt enjoyed the view.

"Seriously, JimBee?" he asked.

Anne shrugged. "His real name is Jim initial B period Toth. When he was in elementary school, someone thought it was cute to call him JimBee."

"And he's let people keep it up."

Anne spread her hands in a "what can you do?" gesture. "I've been concerned about Sarah's home life since last year," she said. Sarah had first taken the SAT in her junior year, and her score had attracted a great deal of attention. "I'd hoped the situation would improve over the summer. I helped Sarah apply for computer camp, which meant four weeks away from home for her, but whoever's hurting her just can't stop. I guess it's time to start the ball rolling." She smiled at Holt. "Not a base-ball reference. I'll give the Toths a call."

JimBee Toth was a handsome man, a bit past his prime. He'd married late, in his early thirties, because (as he told everyone) "I was having a good time screw-ing everything that moved, so I didn't want to settle down." When he'd finally decided it was time to start a family—perhaps when it became a little harder for him to "screw everything"—he'd chosen Lizzy Bell, a blonde ten years younger than him. Lizzy was plain in the face but a hot babe in the body. To JimBee's shock, eight and a half months after they'd wed, Lizzy had delivered baby Sarah. His "hot babe" had turned into a mother, and JimBee was no longer the center of her universe. Worse, Lizzy's figure changed. Her stomach was no longer flat, her boobs were not as perky, and she had stretch marks.

JimBee had had a hard time adjusting to this new situation. A very hard time. He did not love the baby. He felt he should, and it baffled him, until he had a revelation. JimBee realized one morning—following a night when the baby had cried for hours—that Sarah couldn't be his.

Eight and half months? Sure, he and Lizzy had been enjoying themselves prior to their marriage. But what if Lizzy had also been enjoying someone else? That chimed with so many of JimBee's suspicions that he knew instantly it was the truth. And while he never confronted Lizzy with her possible lack of faithfulness, he never loved Sarah. If she'd been an adorable, quiet baby, that would have been one thing...but she wasn't.

Sarah had allergies that kept her indoors, clogged and wheezing and crying. Lizzy was always exhausted staying up with the little brat, suctioning her nose and rocking her, held upright against her chest to breathe. When Sarah was old enough to begin solid food, of course she had food allergies. Then when she was ten, she'd needed glasses, and couldn't wear contacts, for God's sake. The girl couldn't catch a softball, and she sure couldn't hit one. She had to carry an EpiPen, and she got plump, and she had to get allergy shots...the list of strikes against the girl grew with each year.

Though Sarah could read by the time she was four, JimBee didn't think much about that. He figured any girl of *his* would grow up to be a cheerleader, or a

Homecoming Queen, or at least popular. When Sarah had been born, he had imagined it might be kind of cool, watching boys trailing after his daughter, giving her advice on what to put up with and when to shut it down. But Sarah never had many phone calls that he knew of, and she never came to him for advice. He finally had to admit there was only one thing that made "his" daughter special.

Sarah was smart.

She was in the Honor Society, and she got some award for writing a poem. She had a bunch of certificates. And other dads congratulated him on Sarah's achievements, from time to time.

But really, what use was her brain? He sure as hell couldn't afford to send her to Davidson University, which the girl had set her heart on. She could damn well get a scholarship to the local junior college, and he told her so. He was not going to send her to a fancy place like Davidson when she wasn't even his own daughter. And he told her that too.

Lizzy's second child, James B. Toth, Jr., was a son any tire salesman could be proud of. It was evident fairly soon that James wasn't real long in the brains department, but he could play sports (though not brilliantly), he passed in school (though with an effort), and he was popular (in a modest kind of way). The only strange thing about James was his strong bond with his sister. JimBee wondered at this bond and resented it, in equal measure.

JimBee, who cheated on Lizzy—though not as regularly as he would have liked—found himself fantasizing about Anne DeWitt after he'd attended a Rotary Club meeting at which she'd spoken. So when she called the Toths into her office for a conference, he simply didn't tell Lizzy, so he could meet Anne on his own. The principal was a fine-looking woman; and as a widow, she must need some lovin'. It stood to reason.

JimBee was full of a pleasurable anticipation when he arrived at Travis High. When Christy told him Anne was ready to see him, JimBee cheered inwardly. DeWitt was wearing a straight skirt and high heels. Her legs were spectacular.

He was a bit disappointed when she took her seat behind the broad desk. The surface hadn't been cleared for action. There were stacks of paper everywhere, and a metal in-basket that was far from empty.

"What's on your mind, Miss Principal?" he asked, flashing the big white smile that had helped him sell a lot of tires. "I can give you a great price on some steel-belted radials. Real safe driving."

"In a way, it's safety that I want to talk to you about," Anne said. "Specifically, your daughter's."

An alarm bell sounded in JimBee's lizard brain. "Sarah's not sick, not that I know about," he said cautiously. "She'd have talked to her mother about that."

"She seems to get hurt a lot." The principal's expression was neutral.

"She's always been a clumsy gal," JimBee said, his inner alarm bell clanging nonstop. "I'm afraid her brother got the athletic skills."

"Really? Coach Redding tells me all he can do is play football," the principal said. Her face was as calm and immovable as a glacier. "Redding tells me that on the field, James is not good at strategic thinking. He has to be given the same directions repeatedly."

"You shouldn't be down on James because he's no big brain," JimBee said righteously.

"Not like his sister."

"The girl's smart," he admitted. Where was this going?

"She's very smart," the principal corrected him. "She's one of the most intelligent students we've ever had at this school. She's so intelligent she may make a record score on her SAT. If nothing happens to her."

JimBee thought this through. "You mean..." And then he hesitated, uncertain as to how to phrase his sentence.

"No tripping. No falling down stairs. No walking into doors, no bruises, no broken bones. She shouldn't even shake because someone's yelling at her. And that situation should be maintained while she's attending Travis High School. Am I perfectly clear?"

"I can't promise that girl will suddenly stop being clumsy," JimBee protested. "But I'll try my best to make sure she doesn't take a wrong step between now and the test." He wavered between confusion and resentment. After all, he had a right to discipline the girl if he saw the need. That girl and her problems! It was just *me me me* all the damn time. His parents had never hesitated to give JimBee a lick if he needed it, and look how he'd turned out. Whose business was it if he gave the girl a slap every now and then?

"I'm glad you understand me," Anne DeWitt said, though she sounded as if she doubted very much that he did. She stood up, and once again he got to admire her shapely legs, though not with as much gusto as he had before. "I'd really hate to think we might need to have this conversation again."

It never occurred to JimBee that she was threatening him.

That night he got Sarah alone in the kitchen. He said, "I don't know what you're saying at school, girl, and I don't want to have to say this again. You keep telling people I'm beating you, and you'll find out what a real beating is."

Lizzy's daughter just stared at him through her thick glasses. "I never said that," she told JimBee. "Never."

Three weeks later, after the SAT was safely in the past, but before the test results had become available, Sarah was invited to the Homecoming dance by Brian Vaughan. She told her family at the dinner table, her cheeks flushed with pleasure. Lizzy beamed at her daughter, but JimBee said, "Just don't get pregnant. The babies would be ugly as sin."

"But they would be smarter than you," Sarah muttered as she looked down at her plate. Her mother gasped.

"What did you say?" JimBee's tone was ominous.

"I said, 'I wouldn't dream of getting pregnant, thanks to you,'" Sarah said.

"Were you smart-mouthing me, you little bitch?"

"No," Sarah replied instantly. "I would never do that."

"Go up to your room and finish your homework," her mother said. "Your dad wants to watch the football game." Sarah, whose homework had been finished before she left school, left the room hastily, followed by her brother.

"Where's James going?" JimBee asked. "He always watches the game with me. Hey, who's he taking to Homecoming?"

"Mercedes Webster," his wife said. "He's going over to her house tonight."

"She a cheerleader?"

"No, she's the editor of the school newspaper. Real nice girl. Her parents go to First Baptist."

"What's she look like?" asked JimBee, slurring his words just a bit.

"Nice looking."

"He should be dating that Dawn Metcalf," JimBee said. "Head of the cheerleading squad. Her assets were sure bouncing around at that last game."

Sarah came down for a mug of hot chocolate later in the evening and passed between the television and her father when his team scored a touchdown. That earned the girl what JimBee thought of as a light slap.

He was very surprised the next morning to see that Sarah's face was swollen. Lizzy and Sarah left the dining room for the kitchen. He could hear them talking. "It'll go down by Homecoming," his wife said. "Here's an ice pack. You'll look pretty by then. Honey . . . why'd you do that? You had to know you'd set him off."

Darn right. It was all Sarah's fault. And he really hadn't hit her that hard. It troubled JimBee enough that he actually thought about the incident while he checked his Facebook page that morning. No. He really had only slapped her.

* * *

By the time Sarah went to school on a very cold Monday, the bruise had turned to a yellowish-purple color. She'd put on a little makeup, but it was impossible to hide completely. Sarah had pushed up the sleeves of her sweater. Finger marks on her arm showed too.

"Good morning, Sarah. Did you run into something?" Ms. DeWitt asked, her voice calm and low. She was in her usual spot outside her office.

"Yes, ma'am, a door," she said, not even trying to sound convincing. "My dad says I'm awful clumsy." Sarah saw Mr. Mathis noticing. And Coach Halsey.

By lunchtime it had warmed up enough for Sarah and Brian, wrapped in coats and scarves, to sit on the bleachers on the practice field sharing a candy bar.

"I could tell my dad," Brian said. "I hate that you're living like this."

"No," Sarah said. "Then they'd make our family split up. I'd never get the money out of him to go to Davidson."

"I got early acceptance," Brian said, and she bit her lip to keep her bitterness in.

"I'm glad for you," she said, in the steadiest voice she could manage. "I guess it's the ju-co for me."

Brian didn't speak. She was sure he couldn't think of anything to say.

"You remember last year when Teddy Thorndike's family got evicted from their house?" Sarah said.

"Teddy's the one who sings lead in the a capella group? Yeah, sure."

"You remember the guy who evicted them had a change of heart and told them they could move back in?"

"Yeah. Everyone said it was Jesus who changed him." She felt Brian's body move in a shrug.

"I babysat for them. His little girl told me someone had told her daddy they would cut off his, ah, thingy if he didn't let the Thorndikes back in their house."

"Who?" Brian asked her, totally amazed.

It was her turn to shrug. "A secret hero," she said, smiling to show she was half-joking. "Someone who wanted Teddy to stay in Travis so he could do the solo at State."

"Oh, come on," Brian said. "Who'd do that?"

"I figure it was someone here at the school," Sarah said, smiling. "Or someone we see all the time, like our mailman or our minister." She wanted to tell Brian. He was so sweet. She knew he'd never believe her, though. But that wasn't important. "Someone strong and . . . crafty."

Brian looked very skeptical, and Sarah was glad when they spotted Principal DeWitt.

She was speed-walking around the track wearing hi-tech sneakers, instead of her heels. Ms. DeWitt only did her walking at lunch when the weather was cool; Sarah figured she didn't want to be sweaty the rest of the day. After a moment, Coach Halsey came out of the workout room below the bleachers and fell into step with her.

Brian said, "You think they've gotten your test scores?"

"I checked online this morning. Nothing yet."

Brian nodded toward the coach and the principal. "Do you think they're sleeping together?"

"Is that what people think?" Sarah was really startled. It seemed so strange to imagine people the age of DeWitt and Halsey being swept away by passion.

"I've heard some comments," Brian said, trying to sound worldly. "The guys on the team have seen them out together."

"Yeah? Where?"

"At the shooting range. At a restaurant in Candle Springs."

"They're both single," Sarah said, smiling. "Why not?"

Sarah was pretty when she smiled. With extreme boldness, Brian put his arm around her shoulders and scooted closer, and he was delighted when she did not move away.

The next day, Sarah checked online first thing in the morning.

She was only two points off of a perfect score on her SAT. Surely she would get a scholarship to Davidson. She sat, stunned into silence for a moment, thinking about the happiness within her grasp. She ran downstairs.

"I'm sure I can get a full scholarship to Davidson," she told JimBee and her mom. "I know it. Brian's going to Davidson too."

"Slut," said JimBee. "You ain't going to Davidson. You're going to commute to the ju-co."

"You keep telling me you're not my father," Sarah said with a terrible intensity. "I hope that's true." As she ran upstairs, she saw her mother turn to JimBee with the fire of battle in her eyes. Sarah knew, from long experience, that Lizzy's anger wouldn't last long.

Sarah went to James's room. He looked up from tucking in his shirt, and he crumpled at the look on her face. "Not again," he said, as if he were begging.

That morning, a miserable James had to drive them to school. Sarah was in too much pain. She winced every time she sat down.

Two nights later, JimBee was driving home for dinner. It was already dark, because he'd stayed late at the tire store doing inventory. He was looking forward to taking off his shoes, having a beer or two (or three) and eating his dinner. He turned off the road and started down the driveway, rounding the curve up the hill to the house.

There was a wooden crate in the middle of the road.

He screeched to a stop just in time, and leaped out of his car. When he got closer, he could tell it wasn't as large as it had seemed when it appeared suddenly in his headlights. A shove proved that it wasn't heavy either.

"Well, goddamn," he said. Who could have been driving up to (or away from) his house so quickly that he didn't know he'd lost a crate of this size? He gripped a corner with his hands to try to work the crate to the side of the road. Then he noticed there was no address label, and he had time to think, *That's funny.*

Suddenly, JimBee felt a sting. Surely it was too cold for wasps? And surely wasps didn't attack at night? His shoulder burned. He stepped away from the crate, felt his shoulder. In the dim light, he was shocked to see a dart sticking out of his coat. It felt like the time he'd his wisdom teeth removed, though he couldn't think why . . .

And then he felt nothing.

When JimBee woke up he was face down on the road beside his car, which was turned off. His body ached and there was no crate in the road. It was as dark as dark could be.

He hurt all over.

A voice beside him, above him, said, "How does it feel to be on the receiving end?"

"Of what?" he said, as confused as he'd ever been in his life. His face felt stiff when he spoke. Had something fallen on him?

"Of a beating," the voice said.

And then he felt that the other person on the road with him had moved away. JimBee was sure he was all alone in the dark. And he heard his cell phone ringing in his car, where he'd put it in its clip on the console. He couldn't move; it went to voice mail.

He managed to move, finally, dragging himself over to his car, though every move was painful and cost him more than he wanted to pay. *The receiving end.* That was where he was. Though all his thoughts and feelings were bound up in the rapidly mounting pain from various places in his body, he understood (theoretically) that someone had beaten him because he slapped his daughter...and perhaps every now and then, his wife. And just once in a while, his son. But who would do such a thing? The punishment didn't fit the crime.

The next day, as he lay on the couch in the so-called family room—a room no one but JimBee frequented—he had time to ponder the incident. He was full of Tylenol, with a heating pad under his back and an ice pack on his face. He'd wasted a lot of money on a trip to the emergency room, just to find out that nothing was broken. JimBee was so lost in his thoughts he barely registered the knock at the front door and his wife's voice.

"The police are back," Lizzy said as she came into the family room. She helped him sit up. He noticed she was glad to pull her hands away the minute he was upright.

"Bring me some more coffee," he said, not bothering to thank her for the help. He was angry at everyone. Lizzy would pay for her revulsion. When he was better. So would Sarah, who'd appeared shocked by his appearance when he'd finally staggered into the house. James, who should have been swearing vengeance on anyone who dared to lay hands on his father, had simply seemed confused. And they all swore they'd been together in the house since James had returned from football practice at six.

They hadn't even scrambled to the phone to call the police until he'd hollered at them.

And here the cops were, back again this morning. JimBee was getting his taxpayer's dollars' worth.

But after the police left, JimBee was even angrier, and more puzzled, and more anxious.

"We can't find tracks of any other car off the road," Detective Crosby had told him. She was a smart-mouthed woman in her forties. "There's no crate, as you described, in the trees on either side. So we have no physical evidence that you were attacked where and when you say you were."

"Goddammit," JimBee roared, and winced as his whole face hurt. "You think I did this to myself?"

"No sir," she said, all cool and collected. "But we did wonder if you had been gambling on the side, maybe? Or did you stop into a bar, didn't want to mention it in front of the wife? Something of that nature? You say you have no enemies, but this whole scenario seems very elaborate and mysterious."

"I got no enemies, I'm just a tire salesman," JimBee mumbled, his mouth sore and painful. "I don't gamble, except for friendly bets on college football games. Nothing more than fifty dollars on those."

"Are you maybe seeing someone else outside your marriage?" the detective asked, leaning forward confidentially. "Someone who has a boyfriend or husband who might object?"

"Not at the moment," JimBee said unguardedly. The detective's face hardened. Uh-huh, he'd hit a nerve there. Bitch had been cheated on, and who could blame the unlucky man who'd gotten saddled with her?

"Who can you think of who has it in for you?" she asked. "If the event happened as you've described, someone went to a lot of trouble to give you a beating. Someone must not like you, Mr. Toth. Help us out, here."

JimBee glared at her. He hadn't overlooked that "if." But he was genuinely puzzled.

"I really, truly, don't have any idea who did this," he said. Without even checking the clock, JimBee knew he was due to take some more Tylenol. "It happened just like I told you. Believe me, if I knew who had laid into me this bad, I'd tell you in a heartbeat."

Detective Crosby looked at him for a long moment, her face unreadable. "Okay, Mr. Toth," she said, getting up from the easy chair. "That's what we've got to go by."

She didn't believe him at all. He felt like crying.

Lizzy brought him his medicine when he yelled for her, and when he'd swallowed it she sat down in the easy chair the detective had vacated. "JimBee," she said, "you know you can tell me if you're in some kind of trouble." And she waited.

JimBee's eyes watered something fierce. He was touched that she cared enough to express concern. "I got no idea who did this. I can't think of anyone who might have thought I deserved this."

She looked at him, and he could not decipher her expression. "All right, JimBee," Lizzy said. She got up and left the room. He called after her, "Heat up some soup for my lunch!"

* * *

People were talking about Sarah's father after the mysterious beating, and in a way that let her know he was not as universally popular as he believed. She was able to act baffled about the whole thing, and to hide her inner exultation at being right.

With her dad at home moaning in front of the television, she and her mom shopped for Sarah's Homecoming dress and ordered James's tux at the rental shop with a giddy sense of fun they'd never gotten to enjoy before. Sarah picked a long dark blue dress with sparkles on the bodice. She wasn't surprised at all that James selected a completely conventional tux or that he seemed morose. He only began smiling when he ordered Mercedes's wrist corsage.

Unfortunately for the short-lived bliss of the rest of the Toth family, after a week of recovery JimBee felt almost well again. He was anxious to get back to work full-time, anxious to get out of his damn house, and pretty tired of having soup for every meal. Not even homemade! His wife had stocked up on Campbell's. He was bored.

James was shut up in his room every night. When he did share a room with his dad, he looked grim and anxious. And Sarah spent all her non-studying time on the phone with that Brian boy, talking about the Homecoming dance. No one paid attention to JimBee.

So the next time JimBee spotted Sarah walking around with her cell phone clapped to her ear—smiling to herself, like a bitch in heat—he leaped to his feet, grabbed the phone away from her, and hit her in the back with it. She went sprawling.

Sarah screamed so loud that James came out of his room and looked down the stairs at his dad, and Lizzy ran out of the kitchen. Oddly, James looked relieved.

JimBee realized that for the first time he was facing a wall. It was composed of the other members of his family.

"No more," his wife said. Her hands were so tense he thought she might actually swing at him. "You said no more, and I believed you."

"Hey, she asked for . . ." he began, sounding even to his own ears like he was younger than his son.

"Don't you dare," Lizzy said. "Don't you dare say that." She was shaking, not only with fear but with rage.

And as suddenly as if they'd discussed it, Lizzy, James, and Sarah scattered to other parts of the house, leaving him by himself.

JimBee remembered tomorrow would be the Homecoming game and dance. He didn't care if he saw Little Miss Bitch in the damn dress or not. Or even James in his tux. He conceded inwardly that he might go to the game, see if James got something right out on the field.

But that was all he'd do.

Though he'd known for two months that he and Lizzy were scheduled to chaperone the dance, he decided she could do that on her own, if she was so damn mad at him.

The next day, Travis High was buzzing with excitement. The cheerleaders put up laboriously created banners ("Panthers CLAW the Bears"), parents came and went all day decorating the gym and dropping off refreshments for the dance, and though the kids rotated through their classroom schedule, it was easy to see that learning was the last thing on their minds.

"Yes, Sarah?" Coach Halsey said. She'd stopped at his desk when the second period bell rang.

"My dad promised to chaperone tonight, but he's not going to come. Just my mom will be there."

"I'm sure there are enough parents coming, Sarah."

"I just thought you ought to know." She went out. She was walking stiffly.

He related the conversation to Anne DeWitt later that day.

"That's very interesting," Anne said. "I heard Sarah telling Buddy the exact same thing when she came in this morning." Buddy Mathis, Anne's assistant, was a burly plodder who talked tough and looked tougher, befitting the person in charge of discipline.

"Hmmm," said Holt. "Why would she ...?" And then he paused, startled.

"Yes," Anne said. And to Holt's surprise, she laughed.

That night at the Homecoming dance, Principal DeWitt was the subject of many admiring comments. The warm slacks and boots and coat she'd worn to the game had been exchanged for a dressy emerald-green suit and some notable high heels consistent with conservative chic, her adopted look since she'd assumed the name and persona of Anne DeWitt. Holt Halsey (who himself looked fairly mouthwatering in a suit that fit surprisingly well) appreciated Anne's grace as she made a point of talking to all the chaperones working the first shift. The two moms closest to him were talking about Anne. He listened in, of course. "How can she afford such an outfit on her salary?" said a senior's mom. Her husband had just lost his job.

"I don't know, but it sure looks good on her," said a very plump mother, with a sad touch to her envy. "You know, she's a widow. Maybe she got a big insurance payment?"

"Oh, right," said the first mother with some sympathy. "Well, I'd sure rather have my husband."

Not everyone felt that way, Holt thought, and his gaze lingered on Lizzy Toth, who was wearing tired slacks and a creased silk blouse. Holt searched the happy throng for the Toth kids. Sarah was holding hands with Brian, and she looked as pretty as she ever would, with her brown hair hanging free and the dark blue of the dress bringing out her eye color. Unfortunately, the lingering bruise on her upper shoulder wasn't covered by her hair. She was looking around the room smiling, but she seemed a bit anxious. James and his date Mercedes were dancing. James looked like he'd been let out of prison early.

Holt worked his way around the room to stand by Anne. He leaned toward her wearing his public smile, and said, "Well?"

"Seems wrong to let her down," Anne said, clearly surprised at her own conclusion.

Holt shrugged. "Whatever. I can slip out."

"You know . . . I think I'll do it. She's watching you and Mathis. It's about time Miss Sarah got a surprise."

"People will notice your being gone more than me."

"Not in these shoes," she said wryly, and held out one foot, inviting his gaze.

She began easing her way to a corner of the room where a few parents were sitting. She dropped a complaint about her aching feet into three ears before settling herself into one of the metal chairs close to an exit. After a moment, she slipped out, right after asking Buddy Mathis to do a tour of the boys' bathrooms.

In forty minutes Holt saw Anne come back into the gym in a lower pair of heels, reappearing as unobtrusively as she'd left. She drew her change of footwear to the attention of a few moms. "I keep these in my car," she told Lizzy Toth. "They're my go-to shoes." She and Lizzy laughed together.

Holt Halsey completed his tour of the perimeter of the gym, confiscating a flask from a sophomore and reminding a junior couple that public displays of affection in the school gym were not cool before he drifted close to Anne, who was talking to the president of the senior class, a go-getter named Leon Gilchrist. Gilchrist was trying to persuade the principal that he would be the logical choice for Outstanding Senior.

With a few well-chosen words, Anne let Gilchrist know that he was definitely on the list, that his name would be given all due consideration, that she thought he was a good class president . . . and that he should enjoy the dance with his date, instead of talking to her.

"Done?" Holt said, smiling broadly for whoever happened to be watching, as soon as Leon departed to claim his date at the food table.

"Done," she asked, smiling back. "Stairs. He was drunk."

Holt understood from this that JimBee had made an involuntary and very quick trip down the stairs. He had certainly had help, but that would not be apparent.

"Shame on him," he said mildly.

He waited while Anne took a moment to greet some parents who were arriving for the second shift of chaperoning. The first shift parents, among them Lizzy Toth, were easing their way to the door. Lizzy took a moment to crane over the crowd and see her children, with their dates, having their pictures made by the hired photographer.

As Friday night turned the corner into Saturday morning, the gym began to empty out. Holt thought it took a surprisingly long time for the Toth children to get their phone calls from their mother. She must have waited until the body had been removed.

Sarah was so upset her father was dead that she hugged the assistant principal, which Buddy Mathis endured until he was relieved by a friend of Lizzy's. Buddy was glad to resume marshalling the parents who were on the cleanup team. From a distance, Holt thought that it seemed as though Sarah started to walk toward him, but the cluster of solicitous parents moved her inexorably toward the parking lot and a ride home to her mother, sweeping James up into their net. Holt made his way over to the Toth kids' stunned dates, to suggest that Brian take Mercedes home. They were grateful at being organized, and left quickly.

The temperature had dropped on Sunday night, so on Monday afternoon Holt Halsey wore a suit and an overcoat to JimBee's funeral. He was accompanied by Anne, Buddy Mathis, and two other teachers who'd known the deceased. They drove directly to the Presbyterian church from the school.

Buddy said, "Is it true that Sarah's score is the best one a Travis kid has ever made on the SAT?"

"True," said Anne. "I've spent this morning studying the scores of our kids."

"And then this has to happen," said the calculus teacher. "Lizzy is a sweet woman, and Sarah and James are good kids. Maybe . . ." But she stopped short of sharing her opinion that the whole family would better off now. They all understood that.

Buddy Mathis said, "I heard his alcohol level was way high."

Holt nodded. "No surprise he went down the stairs," he said.

"I hope they come back to school soon," Anne DeWitt said. "James doesn't need to miss any classes."

In fact, the Toth kids returned to school the next day. Holt was not too surprised when Sarah came into his class. She seemed much as usual, though she walked with her head up.

In the teachers' lounge that day, Coach Redding told them all how much happier James seemed. "Like the weight of the world had been taken off his shoulder," the coach declared. "I guess it was true, the talk about what happened in that home." He shook his head in a weighty, regretful way. "Them poor kids. Poor Lizzy, all by herself." And Redding, a divorced man, looked suddenly thoughtful.

Sarah followed Holt Halsey into Christy's office after the last bell rang. While he walked straight through into Anne's inner sanctum, Christy stopped Sarah to ask her what she could do for her. Holt and Anne heard Sarah's clear voice asking if Anne was available. Christy appeared in the doorway, barely giving Holt a glance. He'd gotten the impression that Christy did not think her boss should be dating a coach.

Christy whispered, "It's Sarah, whose dad just died? She wants to talk?"

Anne nodded. "Tell her to come in," she said. Christy, after checking to make sure there was a box of tissues available on Anne's desk, went back out to tell Sarah that Anne was ready. Christy tactfully closed the door behind her.

"Sarah, how are you?" Anne asked. Her voice was carefully calibrated to convey a medium amount of warmth and concern. Holt smiled inwardly. "Do you mind if Coach Halsey is here?"

"Not at all," Sarah said. "It's really him I came to talk to." She took a deep breath. "I'm good, better than I've ever been."

Holt and Anne exchanged glances. He felt a little jolt—of anticipation? Curiosity? A little of both, he decided.

"Are you relieved the funeral is over?" Anne said.

Sarah gave her a *Get real* look, loaded with the scorn teenagers can pile on. "He's gone, and he's never going to slap me again, or mock me, or tell me I'm not his daughter," she said. "He's never going to tell James he's dumb, he's never going to talk ugly to Mom, and he can't stop me going to the college I want."

Holt could see Anne considering several responses before she said, "I assume he left your mother some source of income? Or will she need to go back to work?"

"Both," Sarah said with some satisfaction. "Today she went for a job interview as a receptionist at the mayor's office, and she's got an appointment with an investment counselor to keep the insurance money working for us." It was clear Sarah had been giving her mother some advice. Though the girl had said she wanted to talk to Holt, she seemed pleased to have a chance to tell Anne about her new condition too.

Holt reminded himself of how intelligent Sarah Toth was. And how young.

"Is James doing as well as you are?" he said.

"No, James is really troubled, but he'll be okay in time," Sarah said confidently.

"I'm sure what you made James do really bothered him," Anne said.

Sarah's face froze.

"What do you mean?" she said, in a much shakier voice.

"Making him hit you," Anne said. "Much harder than your father ever did."

"James doesn't like to be violent," Sarah said, dodging the allegation. "Like Dad was."

"James doesn't like to hit people?" Anne said. Holt watched her deconstruct Sarah, with admiration.

"Not people he loves," Sarah said. She smiled.

"You told him to do it," Anne said, with no emotion at all.

The little smile was still on Sarah's face as she nodded.

Holt absorbed what he'd just learned. Anne was so sharp. She'd been the best interrogator at the training camp, he'd heard. Trainees would give up their deepest secrets when they'd met her eyes. "Your father didn't beat you," Holt said. "He really did just give you a little slap now and then."

"Even a slap is an assault," Sarah said righteously. "I just got James to improve on the situation." A smile was still on her face. "Dad would never have let me go to Davidson. After I thought about Teddy Thorndike's last-minute rescue, I realized there were a few other kids at Travis who've gotten their way paved, unexpectedly. There's someone helping. I knew someone would help me too. If they thought I really needed it. If I was a victim."

Holt took a deep breath, but decided not to speak. It was one of the few times in his life when he truly had no idea what to say.

"Who did you think this mysterious helper was?" Anne said, sounding mildly amused.

"I don't know. That's why I made sure everyone knew I was being beaten. I thought maybe it was you, Coach. Or maybe Mr. Mathis. Some man bigger and meaner than my dad."

Holt glanced over at Anne, who was wearing a small smile.

"When you're at Davidson, I hope you remember to speak well of Travis High," Anne said, in a social voice.

Though Sarah looked disappointed—perhaps she thought she deserved more praise for figuring a way out of her dilemma—she said, "I will. I'll tell everyone that at Travis, someone goes the extra mile for the students. I thought maybe it was Mr. Mathis, because he left the gym. But he really didn't seem to understand what I was talking about, when I stopped in at his office today."

Holt could see that Anne was not surprised to discover that Sarah had been watching that night at the gym. Sarah'd been waiting, hoping someone would pick up on the hints she had thrown out before the dance. Anne had shown a lot of foresight, getting Buddy out of sight.

"I like to think we do our best for our students here," Anne said blandly. "I'm sorry about your father."

"Someday I'll figure it out." Sarah had the cocky confidence of someone supremely sure of her own brain. "Who helped the other kids. Who helped me."

It was time to squelch this bug. "You will, Sarah?" Holt said. He sounded mildly amused, as if Sarah was discussing a favorite fantasy. "And when you do?"

"Nothing," Sarah said, surprised. "I keep my mouth shut." For the first time, she looked a little uneasy.

"What if someone comes to you and says, 'Oh, Sarah, my mom stole my boyfriend,' or 'My dad is selling drugs to my friends.' Are you going to say, 'Gosh, I might know someone who can handle that for you?' Because they'll be really disappointed."

Sarah stood and shrugged into her backpack. "No sir. Because I'm not going to be here. I'll be in college. At Davidson. And I'll be away from this place forever."

"You certainly have a lot of imagination," Holt said. "And a lot of bravado. What if Mr. Mathis walked in now, and Principal DeWitt and I left? If I believed that someone might have thrown my father down some stairs, I wouldn't risk being alone with such a dangerous person. I'd assume that person wouldn't want to be suspected of murder. I'd know that person might silence me if they thought I'd talk."

Sarah's face drained of color.

Anne stood up too. "Study hard the rest of the year, and I'm sure Davidson will welcome you with open arms in the fall," she said, in dismissal. "Thanks for coming in, Sarah."

Now completely off balance, Sarah paused when her hand touched the doorknob. "By the way," she said, and her voice had a distinct edge, "Darryn Seymour's dad is screwing him."

And then she was gone, closing the door behind her.

Anne and Holt exchanged glances, and Holt sighed. He hoped that wasn't true. Darryn was not going to get any assistance from him or Anne. Darryn was not smart, or athletic, or outstanding in any way, so his attendance at Travis was not contributing anything to the glory of the school. Besides, all bad parents in Colleton County could not meet an untimely end. That would be conspicuous.

"Do you think we need to do something about her?" Holt asked Anne. "It would be a pity, after all the trouble we went to."

Anne smiled, looking suddenly as happy as Sarah had looked. She said, "I'm going to plant a word in the ears of some friends I have left in the business. Let *them* keep an eye on Sarah. I think in a few years she'll be a valuable asset."

Holt said, "That's the best solution of all."

"If she talks in the interim," said Anne, "we'll be right on it."

He smiled at her, and Anne smiled back: smiles honest and open, chilling and feral.

Just the way Sarah had smiled.

SMALL CHANCES

AS I CAME TO KNOW Anne DeWitt better, I realized that what would most upset her would involve becoming the object of someone's pity . . . or ridicule. Her job relies on people taking her seriously. When a smear campaign begins, onlookers are sorry for the targets of the attack. But when the campaign ramps up, that pity evolves and a consensus emerges: there's no smoke without fire. The target must have done something shady to become a target in the first place.

Anne wouldn't like being involved in that at all was what I figured. She'd do her best to get to the bottom of the situation . . . and then she'd do something about it.

The campaign against Anne DeWitt began on a spring morning. Anne was used to surprises of the unpleasant variety: she hadn't been a high school principal forever. The people of Colleton County would have been aghast if they could have seen Anne in her previous incarnation.

But she looked eminently respectable that day, in some very expensive knit pants and a tank under a light sweater. Her fingernails were perfect ovals and her hair was well cut and colored. She was ready to smile at her secretary, who was usually in place by this time.

But Christy Strunk was not at her desk. She was somewhere in the school building; her coffee pot was perking, and the usual pile of messages was centered on Anne's desk. Anne did not like chatty messages. When Christy had become Anne's secretary following the death of the previous principal, she'd been prone to give some color commentary. Anne had quickly retrained her.

The top message in the little stack was dated late the previous day, just before Christy left the office. It read, "Your first husband called. Tom Wilson. He says he will come by tomorrow 10 a.m."

Anne found this curious, since she had never been married.

Anne was not prone to panic. She took a deep breath and considered various scenarios. While she thought, Anne spun in her chair to look the framed pictures on the credenza behind her. The central photograph showed a younger Anne (with a different hair style and wearing blue jeans) and a pleasant-looking man with thick dark hair. Anne and "Brad" were standing in the woods. He was holding the leash of a golden retriever. The young couple were holding hands and beaming at the camera. Even Waffle, the dog, looked happy.

Tragically, Anne's husband Brad had been killed in a skiing accident before Anne had come to take the job of assistant principal at Travis High. After two years of learning the business, she'd been promoted to principal following the (also tragic) suicide of Delia Snyder.

Along with the "happy family" picture, there were three others: one of Anne's younger sister Teresa, who lived in San Diego, and two photographs of their (now deceased) parents: one a studio picture in their Sunday clothes, and another taken at Anne's mother's birthday party, with many candles on the cake.

Anne had never met any of the people in the photos—or, in fact, her actual biological parents. For all Anne knew, they *might* be the handsome couple in the picture. Though she seriously doubted it.

Anne had invented her husband Brad. Now, her created background had acquired a new layer.

Anne felt the muscles in her face tighten as she glanced down at the message once more. This was a threat. She had to ascertain its source.

But at the moment, Anne had to put this mysterious problem aside and take care of her ordinary business. That was what a blameless person would do, Anne imagined.

The other messages were more mundane. One was from the parents of a student who might not qualify to graduate in May. Another was from the school nurse, who needed to talk to Anne about the extensive time she was spending with one student. Anne had also received an invitation to speak at the Newcomers Club, and a request to use the school auditorium for a fundraiser. Anne had to talk to the parents and the nurse, and she noted that. She decided to accept the speaking invitation. She'd approach the school board about the use of the auditorium.

After disposing of those matters, Anne gave herself permission to look again at the message from her "first husband." She found she was quite angry. She turned again to look at "Brad." Over the years, she'd worked out what he'd been like. It had been fun.

"Good morning," said Christy from the doorway.

Of course, Christy had noticed that Anne had been looking at the picture of her deceased husband. "I'm sorry about the phone call," Christy said somberly. She clearly mistook Anne's barely-controlled rage for deep grief. "I didn't know you'd been married more than once?"

Anne considered, briefly and rapidly. She could make up a backstory for this first husband—*really young, didn't know what I was doing, never think about it now*—and Christy would believe her.

Or she could stick to the legend and hope for the best.

Anne made a quick decision. When in doubt, stick to the legend.

"Brad was my first and only husband, Christy," Anne said. "I have no idea who Tom Wilson is or why he wants to see me. Or why he's claiming we were married. But I guess I have to lay eyes on him to find out who he is and what he wants."

Christy gasped dramatically. "Shouldn't you call the police?" Carried away by the exciting situation, Christy offered advice to her boss.

Yes, if I was a real person with no secrets, Anne thought. "I hate to draw that much attention to it," she said, sounding anxious. Anne was sure Christy would enjoy seeing her boss show vulnerability. (Anne was right. Christy was clearly eating this up.)

"Maybe this is someone who's made an honest mistake," Anne continued earnestly. "That's hard to figure out, but I guess it's possible. After he sees me, he'll realize he's got the wrong woman and exit with an apology. Quiet end of a minor problem."

Very tentatively, Christy said, "You don't think...maybe we should have the security guard around?"

Delicately put. "I think that's a great idea," Anne said. "Paul is on today. He should be outside in the hall." It would be a cold day in hell before Anne relied on Paul, retired patrolman, to defend her.

"I'll talk to Paul now. I won't leave the office until this Wilson guy is out of the building," Christy said stoutly.

"Thanks, Christy. I guess I'd better get some work done before he gets here." She nodded at Christy in dismissal.

Christy closed the door behind her. Anne heard the distinctive groan of Christy's office chair as the secretary settled into it.

Anne speed-dialed a number on her cell phone. "Hey," said Coach Holt Halsey. "Anne."

From the outer office, with the door shut, Christy could hear well enough to know Anne was talking, but she couldn't pick out specific words. Anne knew this from experimentation. Nonetheless, she was careful.

"Coach Halsey," she said, "you'll call me a silly bird. But a man who says he was my first husband is going to drop into the school at ten. He left a message with Christy yesterday."

"That's very interesting," Holt said, after a moment's silence.

"Um-hum."

"He tell Christy his name?"

"Apparently, I was married to a Tom Wilson."

"I don't have a class then. I'll be waiting."

"Good." Anne returned to her work, no longer anxious. Holt would see if he recognized the stranger. Anne knew Holt wouldn't worry about her wellbeing. Holt knew her past.

Anne DeWitt (originally Twyla Burnside) had been forced into retirement because of a fatal incident at the training course she'd run, which taught intensive survival training for the best and brightest...which could translate as "toughest and most lethal." She'd been given a new name, a new past, and a job at Travis

High School because there were strings her agency could pull in Colleton County. Plus, the probability was low that anyone would recognize Anne in North Carolina. She had a new nose, a new set of diplomas, a new haircut and hair color, a family, and a very different wardrobe.

After a month in her new job, Anne had loved the challenge, to her surprise. She began laying out her personal program to make Travis High School shine. Her high school was going to be the best public high school in the whole damn state.

There was one obstacle: Principal Delia Snyder. Snyder had not shared Anne's vision. Furthermore, Snyder was involved with a married teacher, and that was bad for Travis High. So Delia Snyder had a carefully engineered tragic suicide.

Anne had many skills.

With her customary discipline, Anne kept her mind occupied until ten minutes before ten. Then she opened the locked drawer in her credenza, removed her purse, took out a Glock and put it in her top right drawer, and returned the purse to its accustomed place.

At 9:55 a.m., Anne switched on a recorder in a drawer in her desk, leaving the drawer partially open.

Promptly at ten, Christy appeared in the doorway. "Tom Wilson to see you," she said, doing a creditable job of sounding calm. She stood aside to let Anne's alleged ex-husband enter.

Anne had been curious to see what her first husband looked like. She found herself disappointed. Wilson was about Anne's height (five foot eight), with sandy hair, black-rimmed glasses, and a slight build. Anne had never seen this man before. Not in this life, or in her previous one.

If Tom Wilson had proved to be a graduate of her training school, she would have had to kill him as soon as possible.

Now she had options.

Christy pulled Anne's office door almost shut behind her with a last, lingering, look and a vehement nod, meant to reassure Anne that the security guard was on hand. The man calling himself Tom Wilson sat in one of the chairs in front of her desk. "No kiss for your husband?" he said. "Anne, you haven't changed at all."

Anne said, "I was only married once, and you're not him."

"You're going for total denial," he said. "Too bad."

"Why claim to have been married to me?"

"That's the million dollar question, isn't it? Maybe I just wanted to see if you'd aged." The smile faded from his face. "You have. I was lying when I said you hadn't changed."

Anne shook her head, thinking about how to handle this.

"You're thinking, *How ungallant he is!*" Tom Wilson said. "And you're right, Anne."

Anne had been wondering if she could break his neck and cram his body in her personal bathroom. With some regret, Anne discarded this idea. "Tom Wilson" needed to leave here in plain sight, visibly intact and healthy. The security cameras had recorded his entrance.

She said, "Who told you to come here?"

"You'll find out," Wilson said. "I've made friends, see? They know who you are."

This was his real face: this small man with his bad James Cagney imitation was mentally disturbed.

While she debated her next course of action, Wilson got up and left without another word.

"I got some clear pictures," Holt said as they walked around the track together. At least once a week, weather permitting, the baseball coach and the principal walked together around the school track at lunchtime.

"Did you recognize him?" she asked, without much hope.

Holt shook his head. "Sorry. But his car was a rental car. He's not a local."

Anne assumed that this whole incident had something to do with her former life. She'd had trouble before with a relative of one of her former students. He'd surprised Anne as she was getting ready for work one day.

No one had ever happened across the body.

But that incident had confirmed what she already knew: it was possible to uncover her new identity if you were very determined and had connections within their community.

"You still in touch with David Angola?" she asked Holt. Angola, who'd come through the ranks with Anne, had been Holt's instructor in the west coast version of Anne's Michigan training school. He'd sent Holt to keep an eye on Anne after Holt had gotten drummed out of his service for his own mistakes.

Holt nodded. "I'll ask him if he knows the guy."

Anne looked up at Holt, a boulder of a man, her hands in her sweater pockets to make her stance look calm. The spring buds had popped up on just about everything. A cool breeze blew her hair around her face. She propped her arms on top of the perimeter fence, and Holt stood beside her, as relaxed as she was. They scanned their kingdom together.

The cheerleaders, now between seasons, were running conditioning drills by the practice field bleachers. Their sponsor watched them like a hawk. Anne spotted a familiar red head. "Madison Bead," Anne said. "Her grade point average is 89. She could bring it up."

"She's not ambitious," Holt said, dismissing Madison and her grades. "Listen, do you want me to take care of this Wilson guy?"

"So much," she said, with an intensity that almost surprised her. "I just can't figure out his goal. He didn't ask me for anything—sex, money, a confession. He's clearly unbalanced. And he only called me Anne. Who could have sent him?"

They resumed their walk in silence.

"He seems to have only wanted to shake me up," Anne said.

"He's done a better job than I would have believed," Holt said. "You've got to stand up to him better than this."

Anne might have enjoyed being angry at Holt, but she understood the sense of what he was saying.

"You're right," Anne said. She noticed Holt's shoulders relax. "I wonder if he's actually staying in town?"

"I'll ask a private eye I know from Raleigh to check all the motels. I'd do it myself, but until we know more about this asshole, I don't want to be on his radar." If they'd been alone, Anne would have kissed him, but the two were absolutely discreet in public. Anne had never thought of Holt as her lover. They had sex and they had a common goal.

At Anne's conference with the school nurse that afternoon, she began to lay some groundwork for the future. After they'd talked about the Lanny Wells situation (Lanny had emotional problems and he had decided visiting the school nurse every day was a good way to deal with them), Anne said tentatively, "Lois, there's something I wondered if you could advise me on. Offer me some insights." The door between the offices was open because Anne wanted to be sure Christy overheard this.

"Of course," Lois Krueger responded, astonished and flattered. Up until now, the nurse's opinion of Anne had been neutral, which had been easy for Anne to read. But Lois sometimes felt that the teachers didn't give her credit for her knowledge; Anne had seen that too.

"This man I've never seen before showed up here yesterday claiming to be my first husband," Anne confided. Lois's eyes widened. Amazingly, Christy had kept mum.

"That's so strange," Lois said slowly. "You hadn't . . . you didn't know him?"

"I've only been married once," Anne said. "After Brad died, I felt that I would never marry again." She looked down, her face sad. "But time has helped," Anne admitted, looking back up with a brave smile. Lois nodded, since the whole school knew that Coach Halsey and Anne DeWitt were going out together.

"Now this man has shown up, making this weird claim, and his conversation is irrational," Anne continued. "Could he be harmless? I hate to call the police on someone who's so ... disoriented."

"You poor thing," Lois said indignantly. "I'm so sorry. You really need to talk to a psychologist, not me, I'm just a school nurse."

"To heck with *just*," Anne said. "I've noticed how good you are with distraught students."

Lois tried to hide her rush of pride. "Thanks," she said. "But really, this man sounds as though he might need to be hospitalized. What a strange fixation! You'd never seen him before?"

"Never. Is that not weird? I have no idea where he came from or who he is. Maybe I'll never hear from him again."

"I hope that's the case," Lois said promptly, "but I wouldn't count on it."

"I'm just glad I've got a good security system at home," Anne said. The nurse patted Anne's shoulder. Anne suppressed her snarl. Instead, she looked brave and worried.

The rest of the day passed quietly.

That evening, Holt stopped by Anne's house to tell her he'd heard from David Angola. No one from David's staff had recognized the photograph Holt had taken.

"But my P.I. tells me that Tom Wilson is staying at a Best Western close to the interstate. And he got into the room when Wilson went out for dinner. He took pictures of everything in the room."

Holt and Anne pored over them. Holt had a second laptop and a second account under another name for just such transactions; he didn't want them on his work laptop.

Just in case.

The sequence of pictures started with a shot of Wilson's rental car. Then the private detective had moved into Wilson's room and photographed an open suitcase, a cheap, black roller bag.

Wilson's clothes were absolutely average: khakis, plaid shirts, boxers, loafers, all national brands and easily purchased at any shopping center in America. Nevertheless, Holt and Anne examined each picture with a magnifying glass, just to be sure.

The first interesting discovery was that Wilson had more cash than Anne would have expected. Of course, there was no way to tell how he'd come by it. He could have withdrawn it from his own ATM. But there was no transaction slip with it, so maybe the cash had been a payment.

The only other subject of the private eye's camera was the inside of Wilson's shaving kit. Disposable razors, shaving cream, comb, Tylenol, toothbrush, and toothpaste. But also, a prescription: pills in the usual golden-brown plastic cylinder. "Why didn't he turn the pills over so we could read the label?" Holt muttered. When they looked at the next picture, they found the private eye had done just that.

The prescription was for Risperidone.

"That's for treating schizophrenia." Holt was grim. "If Wilson is sick enough to be taking it, he's unpredictable. I assumed we were dealing with a person who could appreciate consequences. We're not."

They found out just how unpredictable Tom Wilson was the next day.

Anne was standing in the hall outside her office during the senior lunch period, which tended to be the noisiest. The bell rang, and the oldest kids swarmed out of their classrooms to go down the central hall that ran the length of the school, culminating in the cafeteria. The ninth, tenth, and eleventh grades had all eaten and returned to their classrooms. Getting the seniors to be reasonably quiet as they passed the crossing halls that housed each grade was nearly impossible, but Anne's presence had an effect, especially since she could greet most of the kids by name.

Two of Holt Halsey's baseball players went by. "Chuck, Marty," Anne said. "I'll be at the game this afternoon."

"We'll win," Chuck said confidently. He and Marty paused to talk. Anne was popular with the baseball players, due to her status as Coach Halsey's girlfriend.

Anne's back was to the front doors as she listened to Marty's analysis of the Panthers' pitching roster. So she missed Tom Wilson's entrance through the main doors, his passage through the metal detector without a beep. The startled faces of the boys warned her. Anne swung around, alerted by her survival sense.

Wilson was smiling, his teeth gleaming in the overhead lights.

He decked her. Anne could have taken the blow easily, and it took every scrap of her self-control to keep from leaping on the man and dislocating his shoulders or breaking his arms. But she had to go down, because Principal Anne DeWitt would not know how to deflect a punch.

Anne landed on her back on the linoleum. It was in character for Anne DeWitt to lie there, breathless and stunned. To her immense gratification, Chuck and Marty landed on Tom Wilson like a ton of bricks.

It was all Anne could do not to smile, though she was bleeding from a bitten lip.

The whole school thought it was romantic that Anne had been saved by her own students, and Anne's popularity soared. It was also delightful that Coach Halsey had dashed out of the teachers' lounge and ploughed through the crowd of students like an ice-breaker. Coach had checked that the police had been called (they had, by multiple cell phones), that Anne was conscious and wanted to stand (no, she had to wait on the paramedics, Lois Krueger insisted), and that Wilson was being restrained by the students until the police arrived (there might have been some unnecessary roughness involved).

Tom Wilson smiled through the whole episode.

Holt told Anne that night, "I had wondered if the Risperidone might be a cover, or a plant. But he needs it."

Anne's face was bruised, and her lip swollen, but since Wilson didn't know how to hit, nothing was broken or fractured. She glanced in the mirror and away. *No one likes to look battered*, she told herself. "It took everything I had to just lie there. It was demeaning."

"But way smart," Holt said practically. "You're certainly the darling of the school now."

"That's great, but I guarantee the school board is going to have questions about this," Anne said. "They're going to wonder why this first husband—one I completely deny having married—is stalking me. They're going to think I did *something* to spark this incident. They're going to wonder if he's—by some weird chance— telling the truth."

It was true. Rumors were flying fast and furious through Colleton County. People who'd never heard

Anne's name before were talking about her now. In a very short time, Anne realized she was in peril. Sympathy had swung to curiosity, and then to gossip.

A story like this was not what the people of Colleton County wanted to hear about their high school principal.

"Who would want such a thing?" Anne said to Holt, as she pulled lasagna out of her oven. "Who wouldn't know my original name, and yet want me disgraced or dead? Because if Wilson had brought a gun, I would have been bleeding all over the Travis High floor. He didn't even slow down at the metal detector. He could have shot me from there."

"Someone that crazy...if he knew your real name...he would have said it by now," Holt agreed. "He doesn't know. But who have you scared or angered that much, as Anne DeWitt?"

"Well, Delia was a 'suicide,'" Anne said. "And no one has ever hinted any different. I think that's out. We adjusted Sarah Toth's situation. We fine-tuned a couple of others. What about your ball-player?"

Holt was getting plates out of the cabinet, and he turned with them in his hand. "The last time I saw Clay's parents they couldn't stop talking about what a success Clay is having at U of A. He's not the starting pitcher, but he's gotten on the mound several times. They're in hog heaven."

"So Clay's out. Besides, he never knew it was us." They'd motivated Clay to straighten up his act, so his pitching would lead to glory for the school.

"And Sarah seems to be doing fine at Davidson, according to her mother—who just got engaged, by the way, to Coach Redding." Sarah Toth and her mother had endured a lot from JimBee Toth, until he'd fallen down the stairs in their home while he was drunk. And alone. The football coach would be a much better spouse.

"I heard. What happened to her brother?"

"He went into the military."

"So that's all the Toths accounted for. Let's see what the police say about Tom Wilson."

Later that evening, two detectives came to Anne's house. They had called ahead. "I've seen you at the games," Nedra Crosby said. "We still go sometimes. My husband played football and I played softball at Travis High, back in the dark ages."

Since Crosby was in her mid-forties, that was a slight exaggeration, but Anne and Holt smiled obligingly. The other detective, Leland Stroud, a very dark man with hair cut close to his scalp, was the strong silent type. So far.

Anne offered the two Coca-Cola or tea, but they both refused. "Can you tell me who this Tom Wilson is?" Anne asked.

"Yes," Crosby said. "His prints were on record. His mental problems have landed him in trouble before now. Wilson has just gotten out of a mental health facility in South Carolina. His family reported him missing a week ago. He had a legal driver's license, so he was able to rent a car and check in at the motel here with no problem. He had quite a bit of cash, and a prepaid Visa gift card. We don't know where he got it. His family members all deny giving him money."

"So why did he come here?" Anne asked. "Why did he target me?"

Crosby said, "We wonder that too. You're sure you've never seen this Tom Wilson before?" There came the shadowing of doubt.

"I'm sure," Anne said. Holt nodded in agreement.

"He had some documents in his car," Crosby began. Anne had an ominous feeling. "Including some personal letters signed by you."

Anne didn't have to feign her astonishment. "No, they're not," she said. Anne didn't write letters for that very reason: people could keep them.

Crosby looked thoughtful. "We'll show you facsimiles, and you can give us your opinion," she said. "Can we have some samples of your handwriting?"

Anne nodded. "I'll find some."

Crosby glanced at Stroud, who took up the torch.

"I know it seems silly to ask you this, Ms. DeWitt, but you can't think of an enemy you have . . . ?" He leaned forward, his hands on his knees, looking as sincere as a judge.

Anne laughed. "I wish it *were* silly to ask. Principals do have enemies, Detective. Parents used to back the school administration, but now they back their kid, no matter how stupid or vicious the child is. That seems to be the new idea of showing love. So—yes, there are parents who don't like me at all. But they'd be more likely to slash my tires or file a lawsuit than do something as elaborate as this."

"No one else with a more personal motive?" Stroud asked. "Someone you might have rebuffed?"

Anne shook her head. "If there is, I don't know who it might be."

"This whole situation is so puzzling, especially since you can't think of any reason someone would do this to you," Detective Crosby said. "But please, look through your memory book and let me know if anything comes to your mind."

"My memory book," Anne repeated. She and Holt looked at each other. "I hope you brought these letters with you." She went to the kitchen and got a grocery list and a to-do list. She handed them to Stroud.

Crosby opened a folder to show Anne the letters, obviously copies of the originals. Anne and Holt read them at the same time. The first one began, "Tom, I have been thinking of you every day. I really regret our separation. Please come see me to discuss it? I may have changed my mind by the time you get here, but I beg you to come."

Each of the three letters had a similar message; they all contained the same contradiction.

"No wonder he slugged me," Anne said. "These all say, 'Come here and maybe I'll take you back or maybe I'll reject you.' " She shook her head. "Poor guy. But at least you can see that this handwriting is nothing like mine."

The next day, Anne received a bouquet of black flowers. When the florist carried them into the office and put them down on Christy's desk, she used the intercom to call Anne, who came out to see them. All the flowers had been dyed black, and black ribbon encircled the black vase.

"Who sent these?" Anne asked the delivery woman, who'd already turned to leave.

"It was an Internet order, and they paid with Pay-Pal," the woman said. "You'd have to get a warrant or something to try to track that."

"Is there a card?" Christy asked, taking the words right out of Anne's mouth.

"No. We asked, but she didn't want any kind of acknowledgment."

"She?"

"Well, something she said in the live chat made me think it was a woman." The florist clearly wanted to go.

Anne said, "Thanks," and the woman sped off. Anne took the vase into her office.

An hour later, she knew there wasn't a bug in the bouquet. There was not a secret message, either.

The next day, a young man in a policeman's uniform arrived at Anne's office and asked to talk to her. Though Christy noticed he was carrying a CD player, she didn't think it through, and called Anne out of her office. The "policeman" turned on his music ("Bad Boys") and began his routine. He'd gotten down to his pants when Anne stopped him with a few well-chosen words that really shocked Christy. Anne told him to sit still until the real police got there.

Detective Crosby arrived in fifteen minutes. In the interim, Anne learned that the young man's stage name was Randy Rodman, he had a website, and he'd never had a problem like this before.

Even Crosby had to smother a snigger.

"We can get a warrant to search his apartment, maybe," Crosby said. "Though I don't know why a judge would grant it. After all, sending a stripper to your office isn't a terrible crime. Mr. Rodman says he was left an envelope with a cash tip in it, in his mailbox. A note in the envelope told him the time and place and recipient, if that's what you call it, of the . . . performance. He figured it was for your birthday. I'll check to see if his apartment complex has any security cameras that might have caught the individual who left the envelope, but Pine Grove is low-end. By the way, Tom Wilson is back in the mental hospital in South Carolina. His mother had him admitted again for observation."

In the next couple of days, Anne became aware that there were laughs and giggles when she passed students in the hall. It was all too clear that this series of events was doing what it had been designed to do: make her a figure of fun.

Anne didn't mind being disliked, or even hated. But being an object of ridicule was not only galling, it also threatened Anne's job. She was furious, especially after she got a call from her superintendent. He asked, in the mildest possible terms, if there was anything he should know? Be concerned about?

It took all of Anne's formidable self-control to reply calmly that she herself did not understand what was happening, and that she sincerely hoped that these pranks were at an end.

But they weren't. When Anne got to school the next

morning, there was a banner hanging over the front door. It read, "Anne, I love you. Your Booboo."

Anne called the janitor. He was very lucky he had clocked in on time. Ten minutes later, he had removed the sign and was burning it in the school incinerator. But not before a few early students had taken pictures and sent them to forty of their best friends.

Anne immediately reviewed the security footage from the night before. It showed a figure in sweatpants and a hoodie hanging the banner with the help of a stepladder. There was a knit balaclava further obscuring the person's head and face. "It's not even possible to tell if it's a man or a woman," she said disgustedly.

Holt watched the few minutes of footage again. "I think it's a woman," he said. "There's something about the way she goes up the ladder that makes me think so."

"This has to come to an end," Anne said.

"You're right." Holt was as serious as Anne. "We have to figure out who wants to discredit you."

Anne nodded somberly.

But life didn't stand still so they could concentrate on the problem. It was baseball season, and Holt was busy until late every afternoon and on some weekends.

Anne used her free time to do some spring cleaning (including her weapons safe: the school board would have been very surprised if they could see inside *that*) and finally turned her efforts to culling her wardrobe. That didn't require intensive focus, so her mind ranged free while she sorted and tossed.

This campaign of ridicule was clearly personal. Anne tried to think of anyone local who could take offense at something she'd done; someone so angry they would resort to spending money, time, and thought to playing these elaborate pranks.

She couldn't imagine what she could have done to bring this sly retribution down on herself. If she enlarged the circle to include people who hated her because of incidents in her life as Twyla Burnside, there were any number of people who qualified as candidates. But it was clear that this campaign was against Anne DeWitt.

Then Anne caught at an elusive thought, a shining fish in the water. She stood absolutely still until she grasped the fish and looked at it. She stared into the middle distance, a peach silk blouse clutched in her hands.

What if it's not me?

What if . . . "What if it's for Holt?" she said out loud. She was not just a principal. She was Holt Halsey's "girlfriend." Though that bashful word hardly covered their relationship . . . which was very adult.

"Him, not me," Anne said, the revelation striking her, giving off the ring of truth. She sat on the edge of the bed, the blouse forgotten in her hands, and examined this new idea. After looking at it from all sides, Anne felt certain she was right.

Holt had come to work at the high school a year after Anne, but he'd only revealed that he knew who she was much later. Holt could have done a lot of things before they'd become lovers. Something stirred in Anne, an alien feeling. She'd never thought about Holt's previous amours.

She was going to have to pry.

Holt would be tired after the long afternoon practice, and the Panthers had a game the next day. She could tell Holt was surprised when she insisted that he stop by before he went home. But she told him she'd cook dinner, and a balanced meal during the season was irresistible.

Anne had prepared lemon chicken, rice, and asparagus. Holt was tired, hungry, and preoccupied with his best catcher's bad knee, so they ate in near-silence. Anne didn't mind: she understood being absorbed in a job.

Holt roused himself after he'd cleaned his plate. "What's the occasion?" he said. He was rough hewn and large, but he was also clever and ruthless. Abruptly, Anne realized she was fond of him.

"Holt," Anne said. "I had an idea today about this . . . series of ludicrous events."

"What was it?" he said, looking more interested.

"Who would be angry that you were unavailable?" Anne said, her eyes intent on his face.

Anne had seldom taken Holt by surprise. She had this time.

"Ohhh," he said, leaning back in his chair. "You mean, because I'm seeing you? Someone I had a relationship with before you?" He had to think about it. "Carrie Ambrose," he said after a long moment. Carrie was a divorced biology teacher. "And Lois, the nurse."

Anne held herself still with an effort. Anne wouldn't have thought Carrie would appeal to Holt, since she was what Anne thought of as "fluffy." But she'd been wrong, obviously. And Lois . . . that was really unexpected. "Anyone else?" she said quite calmly.

"Melayna Tate," he said. An emotion passed over his face quickly, too quickly for Anne to read it.

"You had some kind of relationship with these three women?"

"No," he said. "We had sex."

Anne knew Lois best of the three. And she felt that if Lois was dreaming up this elaborate plan against her, Lois was deeper than she'd ever given her credit for being. But the nurse was an intelligent woman. It was possible. Carrie Ambrose had been dating a man in Travis for a while, at least as long as Anne could remember. Melayna

Tate was the girls' basketball coach. Anne did not know Melayna very well: Melayna's team won often enough, the parents seemed content, so Anne had had no reason to observe the coach closely.

"The person in the security footage could be Melayna or Lois," Anne said. "I think they're more likely than Carrie. Whoever hung the sign, she swarmed up that ladder. Carrie isn't muscular, and she's heavier. Tell me about Melayna and Lois." She waited, her hands folded.

"You're too smart to be sensitive about Melayna or Lois." Holt sounded doubtful.

Anne said, "Yes, I am." She smiled reassuringly. "I'm assuming there's a reason you quit having sex with them."

Holt tried smiling back. "Lois is smart, and she has a good sense of humor, but I was not what she was looking for. I think she knew that too. She quit calling. Melayna was wild. And emotional. I had the feeling she was thinking of names for our children. She mentioned moving in with me after two dates."

Anne didn't comment on that. "So Lois and Melayna seem possible, but I should check out Carrie Ambrose," she said. "Whoever it is, she wants to discredit me. Apparently, she feels I took you away from her."

Holt looked embarrassed. "They should know better," he said.

"Whoever. We need to shut her down," Anne said. "Because the superintendent is asking pointed questions. The teachers and the kids are laughing at me. It's going to take me a long time to rebuild my standing."

"If we expose her," Holt said, "that would clarify the blame."

"Principal, coach, and another school employee, caught in a love triangle? Not good."

"This has to stop, and it should be explained some-how. What if . . . what if you weren't the only person she was trying to smear?"

"That would dilute the situation," Anne said slowly. "And take the spotlight away from me."

"So, who's our choice?"

"Let's make it a man." Anne smiled. "What about Ross Montgomery? The middle school principal? He's a douche."

"Ross? Perfect." Holt looked happier by the second. "How can I help? My game and practice schedule right now . . ."

"I understand," Anne said calmly. "You can leave it to me."

Ross Montgomery had a hell of a week. He'd been the middle school principal in Travis for fifteen years, and he planned to die in harness there. He'd gotten things just the way he liked them, as he told everyone who would listen. His assistant did most of the work, Ross could bully his secretary (which made him feel important), and the kids weren't too bad since most of them were small enough to be cowed.

Ross drove into the staff parking lot just before the first bell on a Wednesday. He saw no point in getting there any earlier. As he strode up the sidewalk to the front door, he noticed a clump of students pointing and looking up. Naturally, he looked up too. The banner (which had started life as a white sheet) hanging between the US flagpole and the state flagpole had blue painted writing; it looked the same as the pictures of the one left for Anne DeWitt, Ross remembered. ROSS DATES DONKEYS, this one read.

Ross had had a few belly laughs about Anne DeWitt's problem, along with a lot of other people. Now the shoe was definitely on the other foot.

Though the damn kids weren't supposed to have cell phones, of course some did. Before Ross could confiscate the phones, at least three children had taken pictures and sent them. There was never any way to hide anything now!

In the ensuing week, Ross Montgomery received ten fifty-pound bags of manure, dumped in the schoolyard despite his protests. Ross loathed the Clemson Tigers with a mighty passion, which was no secret. He found stuffed tigers of all descriptions hanging from the trees in his front yard when he got up on Monday morning. One was glued to his front door.

Ross called Anne DeWitt later that day. She was the one person uniquely qualified to sympathize with him, he figured. Ross forgot all the sly remarks he'd made about Anne's "first husband," her black bouquet, and the sign over the high school entrance . . . and of course, the stripper. If he expected Anne to exhibit some collegial feeling, Ross was sorely disappointed.

Not only did Anne DeWitt offer no sympathy, she barely responded to his complaints. "Sorry, Ross. I'm really snowed under today," she said. "It won't last forever." Ross didn't know if she meant the work or the persecution.

The same police detectives visited Ross, Nedra Crosby and Leland Stroud. They reviewed security footage of the middle school and only discerned a slim person about five foot eight, swaddled in sweat pants, a ski mask, and a hoodie. The person arrived with a step stool and all the other materials needed to hang the banner, and that was that. Quick in and out, no shot of the face. During the tiger-hanging incident, Ross's neighbors had seen nothing. And the individual who'd paid for the manure had left a note and cash to book the delivery.

The note had been signed in a good imitation of Ross's signature.

The smart-ass remarks and the derision switched from Anne to Ross Montgomery. As all the other school principals in the area realized they could be targeted next, the laughter died down and the worry started up.

After four days, Anne judged the right effect had been achieved.

She'd been gathering information about Lois Krueger, Carrie Ambrose and Melayna Tate, of course, including a look at their employment records. She laid her plans. She would set them in motion the next day, after she attended the funeral of the husband of one of the bus drivers.

Anne was definitely in the mood to tackle a problem. The funeral home director had caught Anne in a corner to urge her to make "pre-need" arrangements.

So Anne requested that Carrie come in to Anne's office to talk about the lab equipment, which Carrie had complained was inadequate.

Their discussion was short and to the point. Though Carrie was not the brightest teacher at Travis High, she knew her math. Carrie could prove that there wasn't enough basic equipment to go around, and knew the percent of breakage every year. Anne agreed to find enough money in the budget to bring the lab up to par. It was a cordial meeting. Anne carefully maneuvered the conversation to cover first husbands, dating, and Carrie's hometown.

"Bowling Green," Carrie said. "My former husband got a job here, so off we went." She shrugged. "But I'm not sorry. It's nice in Travis."

"You've taught in Bowling Green and Travis, nowhere else?" Anne said casually.

"No," Carrie said. "Seven years altogether, though."

As Carrie got up to leave, Anne said, "Didn't you date Holt Halsey?"

Of course Carrie knew that Anne was seeing Holt now; everyone at the school knew that. But Carrie's expression stayed uninterested. "Oh, for about five minutes," she said. "I've been seeing Mack McCormick for a year now. You know him? The manager at Chili's?"

Anne was convinced she could strike Carrie Ambrose off the very short list, unless Carrie turned out to be a superlative actor.

That left Lois Krueger or Melayna Tate. Anne had read every word of Lois's record, and the nurse's office was close to Anne's. It was easy to find a chance to talk to Lois, and Anne felt the time was right when Lois came into the office to report a student who'd developed symptoms of what looked horribly like measles. Lois had called the boy's mother, who'd come to get him to take him straight to the doctor. They'd find out later.

"Good call, Lois," Anne said.

Lois looked at her doubtfully. "Anne, what else was I going to do? Tell him to go back to class?"

Anne had hit a false note. "You're right," she said. "I'm so used to cheering on the kids that it's leaking over into my conversation with adults."

Lois relaxed. In a moment, they were laughing together over Ross Montgomery's takedown.

Anne just couldn't picture Lois doing everything her persecutor had had to do. For one thing, Lois had a child, a ten-year-old girl. That would make it hard (though not impossible) for Lois to sneak around with secret payments or a stepladder.

If the persecutor wasn't Carrie or Lois, barring the discovery of some secret, ardent Holt fanatic, Anne was reasonably sure that Melayna Tate was the woman she was after. Anne could think of no justification for calling Melayna to her office. The basketball coach was popular with her talented team, and she was a competent teacher; more than Anne could say for most coaches.

To make absolutely sure she had treed the right raccoon, Anne arranged for her path to cross Melayna's when they were on outside duty during the senior lunch period. The weather was beautiful, so most of the kids went to the covered picnic table area in the few minutes they had after eating in the cafeteria. Anne wandered over to the coach, who was staring into space.

When Melayna woke from her daydreaming to find Anne was standing beside her, her whole posture altered. "To what do I owe the pleasure?" Melayna snapped. Obviously, she thought better of her words the minute they left her mouth. She looked away, her jaw hard because her teeth were clenched. Anne knew that body language.

It was something of a revelation to Anne, all the feelings that welled up inside her at that moment of clarity.

"I believe I can go where I like in this school," Anne said calmly.

After a visible struggle, Melayna regained control. "I'm sorry," she said. "I was off in the clouds somewhere. You startled me."

"Yes," Anne said, and moved away at a calculated angle. Anne could see Melayna's face reflected in a classroom window. It was tense and taut with strong emotion. One of Anne's instructors had called such an open display of feeling "showing your ass."

Anne strolled away, suppressing her smile. Objective acquired.

Anne called Melayna Tate's previous school at a tiny town in South Carolina. She talked to the principal, a cordial man who knew Melayna's whole extended family.

"Melayna's volunteered to be on the staff counseling service," Anne said. She'd just made that service up. "We just wondered if she were strong enough?" Anne let the question trail off. "Since she was in therapy herself, she told me," Anne said, following a hunch.

"Well, yes," Mr. Sherman said unhappily. "Melayna was a student here before she became a teacher. She had a problem with her mother's remarriage. It took her a long time to adjust to Jay Tate as her father. But she got over that! Then, after her senior year, she had trouble with her boyfriend. He transferred to another college, and she, ah, took it wrong. But getting help is a sign of health. I hope she's feeling well now? I haven't said too much?"

"She's got a solid record here," Anne said reassuringly. "Her name before she adopted the Tate name was Wilson?"

"Yes," Sherman said, relieved. "The Wilsons are all . . . well, they're, ah, interesting people. Very nice!"

That hadn't been the first comment that had popped into Mr. Sherman's mind. Anne would bet good money that Sherman had been about to say, "The Wilsons are all high-strung," or "The Wilsons have had their share of nuts on the family tree."

Of course, Wilson was a common name, and there was a small chance that Melayna Tate had no connection with Tom Wilson, the mentally ill man who had claimed to be Anne's first husband. But Anne did not believe in small chances.

Anne worked out her course of action. She was smiling. That night, in the dark, Anne left her house.

The Travis Panthers had a home game the next afternoon. Anne was in the stands, as usual. Melayna was there too, perhaps because she could sit and watch Holt Halsey for a long time without anyone noticing.

Anne watched Melayna, perfecting her plan as she did so.

That night, around one a.m., Anne again crept into Melayna's yard. She'd parked a mile away. She was wearing dark clothes, but not all black, just in case she was stopped. She didn't want to look like a secret creeping ninja. She had prepared a backup story involving a broken down car, a lost cell phone, and her need to find the nearest person she knew for help. She could sell it, but she didn't want to be obliged to do that.

Much better to be unseen.

Anne was uniquely qualified to do that. She enjoyed employing the craft she'd once taught others. She hadn't realized how confined she'd felt, being in the public sight all the time, being Anne. She paused beneath a large magnolia, safe from observation. She allowed herself to relax and revel in being Twyla again. But then she thought of how Melayna had made a fool of Anne. And she had coveted Holt.

I'll kill her, Anne thought. *To hell with the plan.* The reckless joy she felt was as pure an emotion as she possessed.

Anne had told Holt that she was not jealous, and she had thought she meant it.

She'd been lying.

It wasn't that Holt had had sex with Melayna Tate. That was immaterial. It was that Melayna presumed to think she had a prior claim on Anne's man.

Anne closed her eyes and breathed deep. This was no time to go off track. She recognized her conflict, dealt with it, controlled it. She would stick to the plan. When Anne was sure she'd regained her control, she proceeded.

Melayna had no security system. She lived in a home built around 1950. Though the windows were stiff and noisy, the back door was easy to finagle, for someone with Anne's skills. Anne swept through the small house like a dark wind. She knew the floor plan well. She'd scouted the house the previous night. She moved silently into Melayna's bedroom.

After checking to make sure Melayna was soundly asleep, Anne propped something up against the alarm clock on the night table.

* * *

The next day, Melayna Tate was late for her first class. When she arrived at the school, she was not only disheveled, but distracted. She jumped at any sudden noise, and she couldn't seem to concentrate on her players at practice. Melayna asked Coach Jennifer Lee if she could spend the night at Lee's house.

After a couple of days, the basketball coach was a little better. She resumed sleeping at home, but she got new locks and a security system.

After a month, rumors circulated that Miss Tate had applied for two jobs elsewhere in the state, one at Travis's chief rival, Powell High.

A week later, when Melayna caught Holt alone in his small office, she said, "You haven't even congratulated me on my move for next year."

"You took a job somewhere else?"

"Yeah, at Powell. This is my last semester here."

"Best of luck," Holt said, with a polite smile, and went back to his computer.

Melayna made a noise like a sob when she walked away. But Holt did not look up.

"She felt pretty bad," Holt concluded, when he was telling the story to Anne. They were eating dinner at Holt's townhouse condo. He'd volunteered to grill.

"She should have," Anne said. "She thought it out and hit me where it hurt."

"You haven't told me what you did to scare her so badly." Holt turned to Anne, with a platter of barbecued chicken and grilled corn.

"I left a picture of her sleeping in her bed that I'd taken the night before," Anne said. "And a pre-need contract from First Memorial Funeral Home." Anne smiled, the smile of a shark. "I filled it out with her name, and included her date of death. Which was this coming May on the last day of school."

Holt shook his head and laughed. "Good call."

"I figured there was no chance she wouldn't understand that," Anne said serenely. "Not even a small one."

SMALL SIGNS

A REMARK BY THE PRODUCER for the Midnight, Texas *television series sparked this story. David Janollari is a big fan of the Anne DeWitt stories, and he told me he really wanted to find out more about David Angola. I was taken aback. After giving Holt's former boss a cool name, I had completely forgotten about him.*

Why would Angola show up in Colleton County? He wouldn't be there for work-related matters as Holt and Anne are no longer his employees. He'd have to have some time on his hands. Perhaps he was on sabbatical for reasons that would provide the foundation for an intriguing story. And suddenly I saw a way to tie everything together and reveal a new dimension in the relationship between Anne and Holt.

D avid Angola was leaning against Anne DeWitt's car in the Travis High School parking lot. The bright early-fall sun shone on his newly shaved dark head. It was four-thirty on a Friday afternoon, and the lot was almost empty.

Anne did not get the surprise David had (perhaps) intended. She always looked out the window of her office after she'd collected her take-home paperwork.

Anne hadn't stayed alive as long as she had by being careless.

After a few moments of inner debate, she decided to go home as usual. She might as well find out what David wanted. Anne was utterly alert as she walked toward him, her hand on the knife in her jacket pocket. She was very good with sharp instruments.

"I come in peace," he called, holding out his hands to show they were empty. His white teeth flashed in a broad smile.

The last time Anne had seen David they'd been friends, or at least as close to friends as they could be. But that had been years ago. She stopped ten feet away. "Who's minding Camp West while you're gone?" she said.

"Chloe," he said.

"Don't remember her."

"Chloe Montgomery," he said. "Short blond hair? Six feet tall?"

"The one who went to Japan to study martial arts?"

David nodded.

"I didn't like her, but you obviously have a different opinion." Anne was only marking time with the conversation until she got a feel for the situation. She had no idea why David was here. Ignorance did not sit well with her.

"Not up to me," David said.

Anne absorbed that. "How could she not be your choice? Last I knew, you were still calling the shots."

For the past eight years, David Angola had been the head of Camp West, a very clandestine California training facility specializing in survival under harsh conditions . . . and harsh interrogation.

Anne had been his opposite number at Camp East,

located in the Allegheny Mountains. Since the training was so rigorous, at least every other year a student didn't survive. This was the cost of doing business. However, a senator's daughter had died at Camp East. Anne had been fired.

"I was calling the shots until there were some discrepancies in the accounts." David looked away as he said that.

"You got fired over a decimal point?" Anne could scarcely believe it.

"Let's call it a leave of absence while the situation's being investigated," he said easily. But his whole posture read "tense" to Anne, and that contrasted with his camouflage as an average citizen. David always blended in. Though Anne remembered his taste as leaning toward silk T-shirts and designer jeans, today he wore a golf shirt and khakis under a tan windbreaker. Half the men in North Carolina were wearing some version of the same costume.

Anne considered her next question. "So, you came here to do what?"

"I couldn't be in town and not lay eyes on you, darlin'. I like the new nose, but the dark hair suited you better."

Anne shrugged. Her hair was an unremarkable chestnut. Her nose was shorter and thinner. Her eyebrows had been reshaped. She looked attractive enough. The point was that she did not look like Twyla Burnside. "You've seen me. Now what?"

"I mainly want to see my man," David said easily. "I thought it was only good sense to check in with you first."

Anne was not surprised that David had come to see his former second-in-command, Holt Halsey. David had sent Holt to keep an eye on Anne when she'd gotten some death threats . . . at least, that was the explanation Holt had given Anne. She'd taken it with a pinch of salt.

"So go see him." Anne glanced down at her watch. "Holt should have locked up the gym by now. He's probably on his way home. I'm sure you have his address." Aside from that one quick glance, she'd kept her eyes on David. His hands were empty, but that meant nothing to someone as skilled as he was. They'd both been instructors before they'd gotten promoted.

David straightened up and took a step toward his car, a rental. "I hated to see you get the ax. Cassie's not a patch on you."

"Water under the bridge," Anne said stiffly.

"Holt had a similar issue," David said casually. Apparently, he was fishing to find out if Anne knew why Holt had left Camp West.

Anne didn't, and she'd never asked. "What is this really about, David?"

"I'm at loose ends. I haven't taken a vacation in two years. I'm always at the camp. But until they find out who actually took the money, they don't want me around. I didn't have anything to do. So I came to see Greg. Holt."

That wasn't totally ridiculous. "I think he'll be glad to see you," Anne said. "When will you know the verdict?"

"Soon, I hope. There's an independent audit going on. It'll prove I'm innocent. You know me. I always had a lot of trouble with the budgeting part of my job. Holt did most of the work. Makes it more of a joke, that Oversight thinks I'm sophisticated enough to embezzle."

"That's Oversight's job, to be suspicious." Embezzling. No wonder David had taken a trip across the country. You didn't want to be in Oversight's crosshairs if the news was bad.

"Okay, I'm on my way," he said, slapping the hood of his white Nissan.

"Have a good visit," Anne said.

"Sure thing." David straightened and sauntered to his rental car. "Holt's place is close?"

"About six miles south. It's a small complex on the left, all townhomes. Crow Creek Village. He's number eight."

"Has he taken to North Carolina?"

"You can ask him," she said, smiling pleasantly. Would this conversation never end?

He nodded. "Good to see you ... Anne."

Anne watched until David's car was out of sight. Then she allowed herself to relax. She pulled her cell phone from her purse and tapped a number on speed dial.

"Anne," Holt said. "I was ..."

"David Angola is here," she said. "He was waiting for me when I came out of the school."

Holt was silent for a moment. "Why?"

"He says they asked him to leave the camp while the books are being audited. Money's missing. He's on his way to see you."

"Okay." Holt didn't sound especially alarmed or excited.

They hung up simultaneously.

Anne wondered if Holt was worried about this unexpected visit. Or maybe he was simply happy his former boss was in town.

Maybe he'd even known David was coming, but Anne thought not. *I've fallen into bad habits. I felt secure. I quit questioning things I should have questioned.* Anne was more shaken than she wanted to admit to herself when she entertained the thought Holt might have been playing a long game.

The short drive home was anything but pleasant.

Anne's home was on an attractive cul-de-sac surrounded by a thin circle of woodland. She'd never had
a house before, and she'd looked at many places before
she'd picked this two-story red brick with white trim.
It was somewhat beyond her salary, but Anne let it be
understood that the insurance payout from her husband's death had formed the down payment.

Anne noted with satisfaction that the yard crew had
come in her absence. The flowerbeds had been readied
for winter. She'd tried working outside—it seemed so
domestic, so in character for her new persona—but it
had bored her profoundly.

Sooner or later the surrounding area would all be
developed. But for now, the woods baffled the sound
from the nearby state road. The little neighborhood was
both peaceful and cordial. None of the homeowners
were out in their front yards, though at the end of the
cul-de-sac, a couple of teenage boys were shooting hoops
on their driveway.

The grinding noise of the garage door opening
seemed very loud. Anne eased in, parking neatly in half
of the space. She'd begun leaving the other side open for
Holt's truck.

There was a movement in the corner of her eye.
Anne's head whipped around. Someone had slipped in

with the car and run to the front of the garage, quick as a cat. The intruder was a small, hard woman in her forties with harshly dyed black hair.

Anne thought of pinning the woman to the garage wall. But the intruder was smart enough to stand off to the side, out of the path of the car, and also out of the reach of a flung-open door.

This was Anne's day for encountering dangerous people.

The woman pantomimed rolling down a window, and Anne pressed the button.

"Hello, Cassie," Anne said. "What a surprise."

"Lower the garage door. Turn the engine off. Get out slowly. We're going inside to talk."

There was a gun in Anne's center console: but by the time she'd extracted it, Cassie would have shot her. At least the knife was still in Anne's pocket.

"Hurry up!" Cassie was impatient.

Anne pressed the button to lower the garage door. Following Cassie's repeated instructions, Anne put the car in park and turned it off. She could not throw her knife at the best angle to wound Cassie. There was no point delaying; she opened the car door and stood.

"It's been a long time." Cassie looked rough. Anne's former subordinate had never worn makeup, and she certainly hadn't gotten that dye job in any salon.

"Not long enough," Cassie said. She pushed her hood completely off her head. Dark hoodie, dark sweatpants. Completely forgettable.

"If you don't want to talk to me, why are you here? Why the ambush?"

"We need to have a conversation. I figured you'd shoot first and ask questions later," Cassie said. "All things considered."

"Considering you threw me under the bus?"

When Senator Miriam Epperson's daughter had died in the mountain survival test, Cassie had laid the blame directly on Anne's shoulders. At the time, Anne had thought that strategy was understandable, even reasonable. It didn't matter that Cassie had been the one who'd kept telling Dorcas Epperson to suck it up when the girl claimed she was ill. Anne clearly understood that the buck would stop with her, because she was in charge of Camp East. There was no need for both of them to go down.

Understanding Cassie's motivation did not mean Anne had forgotten.

"It was my chance to take charge," Cassie said. "Let's go in the house. Get out your keys, then zip your purse."

"So why aren't you at the farm on this fine day? Snow training will begin in a few weeks," Anne said. She unlocked the back door and punched in the alarm code. She walked into the kitchen slowly, her hands held out from her side.

From behind her, Cassie said, "Have you seen David Angola lately?"

Anne had expected that question. She kept walking across the kitchen and into the living room. She bypassed the couch and went to the armchair, her normal seat. She turned to face Cassie. "I'd be more surprised to see David than I am to see you, but I'd be happier. He's still running Farm West?"

"He was," Cassie said. She was savagely angry. "We're both on probation until ... never mind. I figured he'd head here, since you're such a *favorite* of his. I just found out Greg is here too. He was always David's man, to the bone."

"Surely that's a melodramatic way to look at it?" And inaccurate. Holt was his own man. At least Anne had believed so.

Now she was leaving margin for error.

"I don't know why both of you are living new lives here," Cassie said. "In the same town. In North Carolina, for God's sake. No two people have ever been placed together."

"Most people get dead," Anne said. "The point of being here is that my location is secret."

"It took some doing to find out," Cassie said. "But by the usual means, I discovered it." She smiled, very unpleasantly.

"Coercion? Torture? Sex?" Anne added the last option deliberately. Cassie didn't answer, but she smiled in a smug way. Sex it was.

That's a leak that needs to be plugged, Anne noted. She should have taken care of it the first time someone from her past had shown up in her house and tried to kill her. At the time, Anne had dismissed it as a one-off, a past enemy with super tracking ability and a lot of funds. Now she knew there was someone who was talking. A weak person, but one who had access to records . . .

"Gary Pomeroy in tech support," Anne said, making an informed guess. Cassie's eyes flickered. *Bingo.*

"Doesn't make any difference, does it?" Cassie now stood in front of the couch, still on guard, a careful distance away. She gestured with the gun. "Strip. Throw each garment over to me."

Anne was angry, though it didn't show on her face. *No one can tell me to strip in my own house,* she thought. But what she said was, "What are we going to talk about?" She stepped out of her pumps and unzipped her pants.

"Where Angola hid the money," Cassie said.

"You'll have to tell me what you're talking about," Anne said. "I'm totally out of the loop." Anne's jacket came off (her knife in its pocket), then her blouse. When she was down to her bra and underpants, she turned in a circle to prove there was nothing concealed under them. "So, what money?"

Her eyes fixed on Anne, Cassie ran the fingers of her left hand over every garment, tossing the jacket behind the couch when she felt the knife. "Someone in accounting sent up a flare," she said. "After that, the accountants settled in. Like flies on a carcass." Cassie waved her gun toward an easy chair. After Anne sat, Cassie tossed Anne's pants and blouse back within her reach. While Anne got dressed, keeping her movements slow and steady, Cassie sat on the couch, still too wary and too far away for a successful attack.

"Both camps got audited?" Anne said, buttoning up her blouse.

"Yes, the whole program. Our accounts got frozen. Everyone was buzzing. Bottom line, in the past few years over half a million dollars vanished."

Anne was surprised at the modesty of the amount. It wasn't cheap to run clandestine training facilities staffed with expert instructors, much less to keep a fully staffed and equipped infirmary. "The money was missing from the budget? Or from the enemy fund?"

"The fund." Both farms contributed to a common pool of money confiscated—or stolen outright—from criminals of all sorts, or from people simply deemed enemies. The existence of this fund was known only to the upper managers and to Oversight . . . and, because it couldn't be helped, a high-clearance branch of the tech team responsible for data handling also had access to the figures.

Cassie continued, "It would have been too obvious if it had only disappeared from David's allocation. It came from the undivided fund. Oversight's pretending they suspect David. I know they really think I did it. *I'm* suffering for it. Even when I'm cleared, and I will be, and get reinstated . . . they've halved the number of trainees for next year because of the deficit. I'll have to let two instructors go."

This was not a novel situation. A money crunch had happened at least two times during Anne's tenure. "Consolidating the camps would save a lot of money," Anne said, because that had been the rumor every time a pinch had been felt. She'd scored a direct hit, from the way Cassie's face changed. Cassie was the younger administrator; she'd be the one to go if the camps combined.

"Not going to happen," Cassie said.

Anne knew denial when she saw it. "What do you think I can do about this?"

"David and I are both on suspension until the money

is tracked down. I'm sure David will come to see Greg. They're thick as thieves. Maybe literally."

"I've been here for four years, Holt for two," Anne said. "It's hard to see how either of us could be responsible." *But it's not impossible,* she thought. "What do you plan to do if you find David?"

Cassie didn't answer that. "I'll find him. Are you telling me the truth? You haven't seen him?"

"That's what I said." Why would Cassie expect Anne to tell the truth?

"What's Greg's new name?"

"Holt Halsey. Baseball coach." Anne could see no need to keep the secret. She planned to make sure Cassie never told anyone.

"As soon as it's dark we're going to pay *Coach Halsey* a little visit," Cassie said. She sat back on the couch and fell silent. But she stayed vigilant.

Anne had plenty to think about. She'd grown into her new identity. She'd become proficient in making her school the best it could be . . . though sometimes through very unconventional methods. She found it intolerable to believe she was on the brink of losing it all.

Anne was mapping out possible scenarios, imagining various contingencies, and (most importantly) planning an unannounced visit to Gary Pomeroy as soon as she could spare the time.

Assuming she had any left. Cassie was an emotional wreck, but she was also dangerous and capable.

It would be dark in less than an hour. Anne figured Cassie planned her move—whatever it was—for after dark. But that left an hour she'd have to spend in Cassie's company. "Want to play cards?" Anne asked. "More to the point, do you want me to touch up your roots? Jesus, girl, go to a salon."

"Shut up, Twyla."

"Did you fly into Raleigh-Durham? Surely you didn't drive all the way?" It was remotely possible Cassie had driven her personal vehicle all the way from Pennsylvania.

Cassie looked at her in stony silence.

It had been worth a try. Anne did not speak again, but she wasn't idle. She had a lot to plan. A lot to lose. There were weapons here in her living room if she could reach them. She counted steps to each one. Each time she came up just a little short.

"That your family?" Cassie said, and Anne's mind snapped to the present. Cassie waved her gun at the set of pictures on a narrow table against the wall. The table looked like a family heirloom, maybe passed down from the fifties.

"Yes," Anne said.

"Your mom and dad?"

"Someone's mom and dad."

"Where'd they find the guy posing as your husband? He looks familiar." Cassie was looking at a picture of Anne and her husband, standing in the fall woods, a golden retriever on a leash. His arm was around Anne's shoulders. Both were smiling; maybe the dog was too.

"He's in the acting pool." Actors came in very handy in training exercises.

"Was the dog from the acting pool too?" Cassie tilted her head toward the framed picture.

"Waffle," Anne said. "The cook's dog."

"How'd your husband die?"

"Skiing accident." That had been Anne's choice.

"Who's the girl?"

Anne had a studio portrait of a young woman on the credenza in her office, so she'd picked an informal shot of the same woman to place in her home. The woman looked not unlike Anne, and she was wearing nurse's scrubs and holding a plaque. (She'd been named nurse of the year.) "That's my sister, Teresa," Anne said. "She lives in San Diego."

Cassie looked at Anne with a mixture of incredulity and distaste. She said, "At my job I can be who I am. I don't have to fake a family. And no one underestimates me. How can you stand being here with civilians? Being *less*?"

"But I'm not less," Anne said. Anne had never thought of herself as a "civilian," the instructors' term for non-combatants. Anne was still a fighter and strategist. Her regime at the school was sure, focused, and covertly ruthless; very much Anne, no matter what name she was using. She could have told Cassie about the gradual improvement in the school grade point average, the better win-to-loss ratio of the school teams. (Except girls' volleyball, Anne remembered; she had to do something about Melissa Horvath, the volleyball coach.)

Anne locked away her concerns with Melissa Horvath. She might not be around to correct the volleyball coach. She couldn't discount the danger of her situation.

Cassie was obviously pleased to have her former boss at her mercy. That came as no surprise to Anne; Cassie had always wanted to be top dog (or top bitch). She'd never been good at hiding that. She'd waited for the death of Dorcas Epperson, one cold night in a marsh. Then she'd seized her opportunity.

"Did you take care of Epperson?" Anne asked. It was a new possibility, one she hadn't considered before.

"No," Cassie said, outraged.

Anne thought, *She means it. She wanted to get rid of me, but she didn't plan the death that brought me down. Idiot.*

Anne's cell phone rang.

"You can get it," Cassie said after a moment. "No cry for help, or you're dead."

Anne nodded. Moving slowly, she rose to go to the kitchen counter. She pulled her phone from her purse. There was a gun hidden not two feet away, and this might be as close as Anne would get to a weapon. But Cassie had stood and was facing Anne, on the watch.

"Hello," Anne said. She'd seen the caller ID; she knew who it was.

"Are we still on for tonight?" Holt's voice was cautious.

Anne had been expecting this call since the clock had read 5:30.

Anne was never late.

"I'm so sorry, I have to cancel," she said evenly. "I've had an unexpected visitor. I don't get to see her often, so we plan to spend the evening catching up."

After a moment's silence, Holt said, "Okay. I'm sorry to miss our dinner."

"Is it Holt?" Cassie mouthed.

Anne nodded.

"Tell him to come," Cassie hissed.

"Why don't you come over here?" Anne said obediently. "I've got plenty of salad and some rolls. I'd love you to meet my friend." Anne really enjoyed Cassie's face when she said that.

"You sure you have enough lamb?" Holt asked. Anne never ate lamb.

"I've got enough lamb for all of us."

"I'll be right over," he said. "I'm really looking forward to it."

"Me too," Anne said sincerely. She ended the conversation. "He's coming over," she told Cassie.

"You two are on dinner terms?"

"Every now and then." *At least three nights a week, sometimes more.*

"Are you fuck buddies?"

"My business."

Cassie could not control her face as well as Anne could. She reddened. Anne had a very faint memory of an instructor telling her that Cassie'd made a play for Holt when they were both at some planning session. That play had been spectacularly unsuccessful.

Even if Anne had not heard the rumor (she was surprised she remembered it, she hadn't known Holt well at all), Cassie had clearly signaled that she had a history with him, at least in her own mind.

Since Anne had worked closely with Cassie, she'd quickly become aware her subordinate was very touchy about her looks, doubtful of her own sex appeal. It was a point of vulnerability. Anne began to wonder if this search for David Angola had more than one layer. Interesting, but not important.

After ten minutes, there was a knock at the door. When Cassie nodded, Anne answered it.

Holt was clutching a bag of groceries to his chest with his left hand. His right hand was concealed. He'd come armed.

"You'll never guess who's here," Anne said, standing to one side to give him a clear shot if he wanted to take it. "You remember Cassie Boynton?"

Holt smiled and stepped inside. "I did not expect to see you, Cassie," he said. "It's been a long time. What are you doing in this neck of the woods?" Anne quietly shut the door behind Holt.

Cassie held up her gun. "I'm looking for some answers," she said. "Are you going to try to stop me?"

"I am," said David, behind her. He'd used Holt's key to come in the back door.

Cassie whirled, but David wasn't where she thought he'd be. He'd moved as soon as he'd spoken. Anne, who'd begun moving with "*am*," leaped behind Cassie and took her in a chokehold. Cassie clawed at Anne's arm with her free hand, and tried to bring the gun to bear with the other.

Holt made Cassie release her gun by slamming her hand with the butt of his own. Anne heard a bone crack.

And just that quickly it was over, without a shot fired.

Anne had broken a finger once (or twice) so she knew how painful it was. Cassie did not scream. Fairly impressive.

"You're unarmed," David said. "You're under our control. If this was a training situation, what would you tell yourself?"

Cassie did not speak. Her rage filled the room like a red cloud.

"You'd say, 'Bang, you're dead,'" David told her. "Did you follow me all this way to try to kill me? Are you trying to prove I stole the money?"

"You *did*," Cassie said. Though they were all liars by trade, Cassie believed what she said.

David's dark face was impassive as he said, "I never took a cent."

"I didn't either." Suddenly Cassie launched herself backward, drawing up her knees to explode forward in a kick that hit David's chest. He staggered back. Since Cassie's whole weight was suddenly hanging from Holt's arm, his hold broke.

With a beautiful precision, Anne pivoted on her left foot and kicked Cassie in the temple with her right. Cassie's head rocked back, her eyes went strange, and she crumpled.

David had regained his feet by then and he was striving to catch his breath. He held his gun on Cassie, but after a few seconds he was sure she was out. His arm fell to his side, and he sat heavily.

Holt had stepped away from Cassie in case David shot her.

"She sounded like she was telling the truth," Holt said, after a moment of silence.

"She did, didn't she?" David looked troubled. "I was so sure it was her."

"She was sure it was you," Anne said.

David appeared both confused and angry. "Do you believe I'm an embezzler? Twyla, Greg?"

Twyla said, "Anne," at the same moment Greg said, "Holt."

"Does it matter what we think?" Holt continued. "One of you will take the blame. I hope it's her."

Anne began to pick up the items that had scattered from the grocery sack. Among them was a knife. Anne smiled. She retrieved her own from her jacket. Then, just in case, she got her gun out of the drawer and put it in a handy spot. After all, everyone else in the room was armed.

She was waiting for the inevitable question. Holt obliged by saying, "What do you want to do with her, David?"

"The options are limited," David said slowly. "We call Farm East and tell—who, Jay Pargeter, I guess?—to come get her. Or we wait until she wakes up, and we ask her some questions. Or we let her go. Or we kill her now."

"We're not part of the system any more," Anne told David, pointing from Holt to herself. "We shouldn't take part in an interrogation."

"You can't let her go," Holt said.

David looked down at Cassie unhappily. "If she was anyone else, I'd put her down. But she's earned some respect. She's done a good job since you left, Anne. Until now."

Holt glanced at Anne and then said, "There's another choice. You could take Cassie up to Camp East yourself."

David looked at Holt with narrow eyes. "Why?"

"Enough people know where Anne is already," Holt said. "Someone had to tell Cassie. If you call from here, at least ten more people will know. Anne, did Cassie say how she found you?"

"Gary Pomeroy in tech support. She also knew you were here, so she figured David might visit."

"Son of a bitch," David said, disgusted. "I'll pay Gary back. Maybe officially. Maybe on my own time."

"If you don't, I will," Anne said. "I don't want to have to start all over again. It seems to be too easy to pry the information out of Gary. At least we'll assume it was him."

"What's that supposed to mean?" David tensed.

"You knew all along where I was. You sent Holt here."

"You were getting death threats!"

"Like that's new. I never believed that's the only reason he came."

David looked at Holt. "So you've never told her why you left?"

"We never talked about it," Holt said calmly.

"We don't talk about the past a lot," Anne said, which was absolutely true.

"Well, *Anne,* you might be interested to know that *Holt* here, back when he was Greg Baer, was suspected in the disappearance—and probable murder—of a doctor in Grand Rapids, Michigan," David said.

"And?" Anne was unconcerned.

"I got tipped off Greg was going to be arrested," David said. "We couldn't let the police come to the facility, obviously. They believe it's a wilderness camp for adults, but if they had a closer look that wouldn't fly. I had to drive Greg into town to meet with them. They'd flown in from Michigan."

"They took me to the local police station and put me through the wringer," Holt said, smiling. "But considering where I work, it was nothing."

David stared at him. "Man, they were going to arrest you!"

"Maybe." Holt didn't sound worried.

"Oversight voted to hide him on my strong recommendation," David told Anne, though he sounded as if he considered that was a mistake, just at the moment. "Otherwise his background might raise a red flag, though I swore to them that Greg wouldn't talk about the program. His background fit the opening here. He had his ears modified and his tattoos removed. A nose job. I figured you wouldn't recognize him right away. You two hadn't actually met, as far as Greg could remember. You could get to know him as Holt."

"You're right, I didn't recognize him." He'd made her vaguely uneasy, though, and it had explained a lot when he let her know who he'd been.

David nodded, pleased. "Oversight charged me with arranging your identities. No one else knew."

"Except Gary in tech support," Holt said in disgust.

"Except him."

"Thanks, then," Anne said. She smiled brightly. Holt was going to have some talking to do after this. From his face, he knew that.

David looked from Holt to Anne. "All right, I'll take Cassie with me. I'll call Pennsylvania once I've gotten a couple of hours under my belt so no one can find out where I started. I disabled the GPS on the rental. It's a seven hour drive?"

"Yes," Anne said. "Thereabouts. One of us could go with you, fly back. You might need help."

"No thanks," David said. "I need to think. Someone took that money. It wasn't me, and I believe it wasn't Cassie. But we both might lose our jobs."

Holt and Anne glanced at each other, quickly looked away. Yes, they needed to talk.

"Where's your car?" Anne asked David.

"We drove over here in it," Holt said. He was staring at Cassie, sizing up her shape and weight. He was a practical man.

"Good. We need to find her car," Anne said.

"Search," Holt said briefly. Since it was possible Cassie was playing possum—though Anne didn't think so—Anne stood a safe distance away with Holt's gun aimed at the prone figure. Holt knelt to search her. In a practiced way, he rolled Cassie to one side, then the other, as he searched her. He pulled two sets of keys from her pockets and stood. "Rental," he said, "and personal."

"She's got a cabin five miles from camp," Anne said. "If she hasn't moved."

"She won't stay out for much longer," David said. "If I get stopped . . . I'm a black man. Just saying." He was saying that not only might he get stopped no matter how carefully he kept to the speed limit, but also that he didn't want to have to kill policemen. But it would be very, very awkward if he were arrested with a tied-up white woman who was screaming bloody murder.

"I have something to keep her out until you get there," Anne said. "You sure you don't want me to come? I could manage her. But I'd have to be back by Monday morning for school."

"You have no idea how weird it is to hear you say that," David said, smiling reluctantly. "I'll take her solo, if she's drugged. What do you have to keep her quiet?"

Anne ran up the stairs to her attic to open her carefully concealed stash of things she'd figured might prove handy. She was a "waste not, want not" kind of person.

"This should be two doses of thiopental," Anne said when she returned. She handed the vials of freeze-dried powder to David, along with sterile water and two hypodermics.

"You keep that around? Geez, Anne. What else you got?" David went over to the sink to prepare the injections.

"Oh, this is a holdover from Camp East," she said. "I picked it up in the infirmary after a trainee broke his leg. I thought it might come in handy some day. I stuck it in my go-kit and I didn't clean it out . . . in the haste of my departure." (In the middle of the night. With two armed and wary "escorts." Not her favorite memory.)

"Thanks," David said. He gave Cassie the first injection. "Is the other side of your garage free?"

"Yes, there's a control button by the kitchen door. You can drive right in. Might as well leave the kitchen door open."

In a few seconds—not long enough to have a conversation—Anne heard the garage door rumble up. She nodded to Holt, who squatted to take Cassie's feet. Anne took her shoulders. Cassie's body drooped between them like a hammock.

David had lowered the garage door and opened the trunk. "I've disabled the safety latch," he said. "I'll keep an eye on the clock and stop to give her the second shot. Four hours?"

Anne and Holt laboriously dumped Cassie into the trunk. It was lucky she wasn't tall.

"Four hours should be right," Holt said. "Sure you can stay awake?"

"Or I make you a to-go cup of coffee," Anne said helpfully. She predicted David's reaction.

Sure enough, he stared at her with ill-concealed suspicion. He said, "No, thanks."

"Let us know when you get there." Holt clapped David on the shoulder.

"I hope they find out who took the money," Anne said.

That was as much goodbye as any of them wanted.

As soon as David backed out, Anne closed the garage door. She and Holt stood in the chilly space.

He was waiting for her to say something first.

"When you were Greg, you had a real family," Anne said. It was not a guess.

He nodded. "Mom, Dad, brother. My father had stomach cancer. He was having a lot of pain. The roads were icy, and my brother was out of state. So Mom took him to the emergency care clinic at three in the morning because it was lots closer than the hospital. I drove from my hotel to meet them there. The doctor on duty was either incompetent or sleepy or both. He gave Dad the wrong drug. Dad died. He would have died soon anyway, I know. And he was suffering. But it wasn't his time, just yet. Mom was sure she'd get to take him home."

"So you took care of the doctor."

"Waited three weeks and then went into his house at night." He smiled. "Snatched him right out of bed and vanished him."

"Did the police really have evidence against you?"

"I'd said a few things to him that night. So they had a lot of suspicion. When they checked into my background, they had even more. And a neighbor saw a car like my rental backing out of his driveway that night."

"Nothing decisive."

"Enough to haul me in for questioning, maybe arrest. David didn't let that happen."

Anne said, "You did the right thing. So did David. Not that you need me to tell you that."

He nodded. "Was that really thiopental you gave Cassie?" he said.

"If I'd had something stronger I would have brought it down," she admitted. "All I'd kept was the thiopental. Cassie might not survive the trip anyway. She was out a lot longer than I'd thought she'd be, and I know she's had more than one concussion over the years."

Holt looked hopeful. "That would make things simpler."

They went into the house. Anne opened a cabinet and brought out a whiskey bottle, raising it in silent query. Holt nodded. She poured and handed him a shot glass, filled one for herself. She leaned against the kitchen island on one side, while Holt sat on a stool on the other. They regarded each other.

"Cancer treatment is very expensive," Anne said at last.

Holt regarded her steadily. "Dad had a long illness. That trip to the clinic was only one of many. The bills...you could hardly believe how much, and the insurance only covered a fraction of the cost. My mom and my brothers were scared shitless. The debt would loom over them the rest of their lives. Mom and Terry, my older brother, think I have some hush-hush military job, and they know the military doesn't pay well. They didn't expect I could help much. They were really understanding about that. It burned me up inside."

"So you siphoned off the money from the enemy fund."

"Yeah. I did."

So there it was.

"You did a good job covering your tracks. How'd you plan it?"

"It helped that David's never been confident with numbers. He always sweated budget time, needed a lot of help from me. I remembered a genius accountant, a guy I'd roomed with in college," Holt said. "Tom was doing the books for a lot of the wrong people. That was how I knew where he was. Tom was glad to help. He's one of those people who loves to beat the system, any system."

"Is Tom still around? Can they interrogate him?"

"He began doing bookkeeping for the wrong people. He disappeared a year ago."

Anne eyed Holt narrowly. "Really?"

"Yes, really." Holt managed a small smile. "Nothing to do with me. But convenient."

"So what now?"

Holt's smile vanished. He looked very grim. "When David showed up today, I felt like the bottom had fallen out. I hated that he was suspected of something I'd done, when he'd done nothing but back me up. As people like us go, he's a good man."

Anne had thought of suggesting they follow David and run his car off the road. She was glad she hadn't said that out loud.

Anne had the feeling they were stepping on thin ice, new and fragile territory in their relationship. The two regarded each other in silence.

Finally, Anne said, "Do you think David suspects you?"

"No," Holt said immediately. "He would have tried to take me out. An honor thing."

"Your family does not know where the money came from. They couldn't reveal anything accidentally?"

"I told them I'd invested money in an online shopping program, and it had taken off. They were too relieved to ask for any details."

"You think Oversight will come back with questions about your dad's bills being paid off?"

"If the bills had been paid in one lump sum, it would be suspicious. But I paid in irregular amounts spread out over two and a half years, some of it channeled through my family's accounts. Less conspicuous." His mouth twitched in a smile. "And I haven't worked at Camp West in more than two years. I live on my coach's salary."

"And the money's stopped disappearing. No one's stealing from the enemy fund now."

"They'll still be looking. No one makes a fool out of Oversight."

"But they might be glad to find a scapegoat."

"What are you thinking, Anne?"

"I'm thinking we can find Cassie's rental. We can drive it to Pennsylvania and get there ahead of David. Two drivers instead of one."

Holt looked interested. "Then what?"

"Then we plant money in Cassie's house, gold or bearer bonds. Untraceable stuff."

"Anne, I don't have anything like that. I don't even have much cash stashed away. Not enough to make them believe she stole everything."

"I have some backup funds," Anne said. She looked away.

Holt leaned forward and took her hand. She couldn't avoid his eyes. "You'd do that?"

"Yes," she said stiffly. "I would."

"No regret?"

"No regret."

Holt struggled to find words of gratitude, but Anne held up her hand to keep him silent. "If they find unexplained money in Cassie's house, David's in the clear, Cassie will vanish, and they'll consider the theft explained. It's all good. I know where her house is, and we've got the keys."

"Let's get on the road," Holt said.

Anne retrieved half of her escape fund from its secret hiding place—the same place the thiopental had been stored—and she was back down the stairs in less than two minutes.

"If we find the rental quickly," she said, "it'll be a sign that we're doing the right thing."

Anne and Holt knew where to start looking. Using the key fob to make the lights blink, they found it in four minutes, parked behind a house for sale on the other side of the street.

During the long drive north, they made some plans for Spring Break.

Those plans involved Gary Pomeroy.

ABOUT THE AUTHOR

CHARLAINE HARRIS is a *New York Times* bestselling author who has been writing for over thirty years. She was born and raised in the Mississippi River Delta area. Her Sookie Stackhouse books have appeared in twenty-five different languages and and were the basis for the HBO series *True Blood*. The Aurora Teagarden mystery series and the Midnight, Texas trilogy have also recently been adapted for television. Her latest novel, *An Easy Death*, is the first in a new series.

Also available from Charlaine Harris as a JABberwocky
eBook or paperback

FOR NEWS ABOUT JABBERWOCKY BOOKS AND AUTHORS

Sign up for our newsletter*: http://eepurl.com/b84tDz
visit our website: awfulagent.com/ebooks
or follow us on twitter: @awfulagent

THANKS FOR READING!